W9-ABH-097

Fame,
Fortune,
and the
Bran Muffins
of
DOOM

Marty Kelley

Holiday House / New York

Library of Congress Cataloging-in-Publication Data

Kelley, Marty.
Fame, fortune, and the bran muffins of doom / by Marty Kelley. — 1st ed.
p. cm.
Summary: Geeky Simon is determined to gain everlasting fame
and glory by winning the school talent show.
ISBN 978-0-8234-2606-5 (hardcover)
[1. Bands (Music)—Fiction.   2. Talent shows—Fiction.   3. Schools—
Fiction.   4. Humorous stories.]   I. Title.
PZ7.K28172Fam 2012
[Fic]—dc23
2011050748

This book is for Kerri, my very own foul girl.

Many thanks to:

My incredibly patient wife, Kerri, who sat through countless readings, re-readings, and re-re-readings of this book as I was writing it. Her decisive, hard-hitting comments, editing, and suggestions were invaluable and helped me make the book better after I was able to stop crying.

My equally patient children, Alex and Victoria, who listened, offered advice, and posed for many humiliating reference photos that I am eager to share with their future children.

My great friend, the amazingly talented musician, Steve Blunt, who gave me insight into the music industry by letting me join his band so I could become a rock 'n' roll legend like The Funkee Boyz.

My terrific, ninja-like agent, Abi Samoun, who rejected the original version of this book and suggested that I change the simple 700 word picture book into a 25,000 word chapter book. Without her, Simon would not exist.

My amazing, super-cool editor, Sylvie Frank, whose enthusiasm and brilliant editorial acumen helped to make this book much better than it was.

Rawrb from Psychostick, Fat Mike from NOFX, and Ben Weasel from Screeching Weasel for permission to use their bands' names on Evil Ernie's shirts. Rock on!

All the rest of my friends and family, who didn't really do anything to help with the book. But I'm glad you're there.

Contents

Chapter 1
The Foul Girl and The Funkee Boyz

I have been trying to develop a glare that will cause people to burst into flames.

I obviously need more practice, because when I glared at Stacy, the foul girl who sits beside me in class, she failed to ignite. Instead, she leaned closer to me and pointed to my secret plan book. "What are you working on?"

"Silence, foul girl," I commanded. "I have an abundance of work to complete and your **frivolous confabulations** serve only to hinder my efforts."

"Huh?"

I thought I had made myself perfectly clear.

"I am busy," I explained.

"So, what are you working on?" she asked again.

"He's probably working on a list of ways that he could be more of a dork," snorted Mike McAlpine from his desk near the back of the room. "But I've got bad news for you, Simon. You couldn't possibly be more of a dork."

Mike's laugh was echoed by his two goons, Evil Ernie and Eviler Ernie.

"Yeah," said Evil Ernie.

"Yeah," echoed Eviler Ernie. "There's no way you could be more of a dork because…uh…because… umm…"

"Because you're hogging up all the dorkiness in the entire state, Ernie," said Stacy.

"That's a good one!" laughed Eviler Ernie. "Oh, no…wait…that's not a good one, Stacy. I'm not a dork. My grammy says that I'm the coolest kid in my whole family."

"Aren't you an only child, Ernie?" Stacy asked.

"Yeah," mumbled Eviler Ernie. "So what?"

Mike dropped his head to his desk and moaned. "Oh man, Ernie."

I turned back to my plans just as Mrs. Douglass trudged through the door, clutching her cup of gray, teacher-strength coffee.

"There are 161 days left until I get out of here," she grumbled. "Now get busy with your work and don't bother me."

Mrs. Douglass's daily retirement countdown is followed by a stack of worksheets that she hands out to keep us busy while she drinks coffee and looks through brochures for condominiums in Florida. She never even collects the worksheets. This, of course, leaves us free to entertain ourselves for the entire morning.

I assumed I would be free to work without **further** interruptions.

I assumed incorrectly.

"Simon," Stacy whispered, holding up her magazine. "Look."

I dropped my pencil and turned to her. "What do you want, foul girl? I am attempting to work and your interruptions are proving **acutely vexatious**."

"Did you just make that word up?" she asked.

"Which word do you speak of?" I asked.

"Um...almost all of them," she replied.

"I most certainly did not **fabricate** any of my **lexicon**," I assured her. "Do you never read the dictionary?"

She laughed a silvery laugh, like the tinkling chimes of a far-off ice cream truck. "Read the dictionary?" she asked. "For fun? That's hilarious. You crack me up, Simon. No, I read this."

She held up her magazine and displayed a picture of three boys posing in front of thousands of screaming girls.

"Aren't they dreamy?" she asked.

I inspected the picture more closely, but could see nothing dreamy about them. "I would not say they were dreamy," I replied. "They look ridiculous in those outfits, and it appears as if their hair has been styled with a lawn mower. Who are those unfortunate fashion victims?"

"Who are they?" Stacy repeated.

Munch looked up from the sticky goo he was eating off the bottom of his sneaker. Munch is one of my associates. His real name is Kevin, but everybody calls him Munch because he will eat anything that he can fit into his mouth.

He leaned forward from his desk behind mine. "Simon, are you serious?" he asked. "My three little sisters know who they are. My three older sisters are all planning to marry them. I think my mom is, too."

"You really don't know who those guys are?" asked Ralph. Ralph is my other close associate. Even though his parents are both doctors, his endless list of allergies, illnesses, and medical conditions has earned him his own private cot in the nurse's office. His spectacular **projectile** vomiting has made him a schoolwide legend. "The waiting room in my parents' office is full of magazines about them. How can you not know who they are?"

"What a dork," laughed Mike McAlpine.

"Yeah," chuckled Evil Ernie.

"Yeah. Even my grammy knows who they are. Now who's hogging up all the dorkiness?" asked Eviler Ernie.

"That would still be you, Ernie," said Stacy. "And,

Simon, these guys just happen to be The Funkee Boyz. You can't tell me you've never heard of The Funkee Boyz."

"In fact," I corrected her, "I can tell you that. I am far too busy with my plans to be bothered learning the name of every ridiculous musical group with poor taste in clothing."

Stacy sighed and began speaking to me as if I were a simple-minded **ignoramus**. "The Funkee Boyz are the most popular musical group in the whole world. And they're super-cute, too. Everybody on the planet knows about them."

"Everybody except Mr. Dork-o-Rama here," sneered Mike.

Munch pulled his finger from his nose and held it toward Mike's face. "Hey, Mike. Does this booger look like Ernie to you?"

"AAAAHHH!!" screamed Mike, toppling from his chair. "Get that thing away from me!!"

Mrs. Douglass slapped her brochure down and glared at Mike. She was unable to make him burst into flames. Her glare is in need of improvement, as well. "What is the meaning of this, Mr. McAlpine?"

"Munch was going to put a booger on me!" wailed Mike.

Munch licked his finger and held his hands up so Mrs. Douglass could see them. "I have no idea what Mike is talking about, Mrs. Douglass. I've just been sitting here doing my work."

Mrs. Douglass sighed deeply. "If there are any

more outbursts, Mr. McAlpine, you'll be taking a trip to Mr. Tappet's office."

Mike quickly sat down and the class was silent.

I continued working on my plan until Mr. Tappet's voice shattered the silence.

Chapter 2
And Now This Brief Message From the Office

"All right. Listen up," barked Mr. Tappet over the intercom. "Mrs. Meredith has some kind of announcement or something she wants to make. So zip your lips and listen up!"

"Um...thank you, Mr. Tappet," squeaked Mrs. Meredith's voice over the speakers. "Is this on? Am I doing this right? Can they hear me?"

There were a few rustling noises and Mr. Tappet said, "Yeah. Just push that button while you talk."

"This one?" asked Mrs. Meredith.

"NO!" barked Mr. Tappet.

There was a loud popping noise and the intercom went dead. A few seconds later, it snapped back to life.

"Oh, I see. Thank you," said Mrs. Meredith. "Well, good morning, boys and girls. Isn't it a wonderful day?" There was a long pause, then Mrs. Meredith said, "Why aren't they answering me, Mr. Tappet?"

"The intercom only works one way, Mrs. Meredith. They can hear you. You can't hear them."

"Oh. Yes, of course. How silly of me. How will I know that they are listening?"

"LISTEN UP!" boomed Mr. Tappet. "They're listening."

"Thank you, Mr. Tappet. Well, good morning, boys and girls. Isn't it a wonderful day? I'm sure you're all saying yes, because it is a wonderful day. And to add to the day's wonderfulness, I have an exciting announcement to make. I am organizing the school's first talent show! Isn't that wonderful? Isn't it? Oh, I can't hear you, but I'm sure you are saying it's wonderful.

"This will be a chance for all of you talented little darlings to show off what you can do. Do you sing? Do you dance? Can you do magic? Juggle? Tell jokes? Now you can show off your talent in front of the whole school.

"The talent show will be held on Friday to celebrate Lunch Lady Appreciation Day. I know it's short notice, but I'm sure that you wonderful, talented children will be able to do amazing things! And there are some wonderful prizes for our most talented students. So come to the gym at lunch to sign up your act, and I hope to see you all at the show! Thank you."

"GET BACK TO WORK!" barked Mr. Tappet.

Everyone in our class began yammering excitedly about the talent show. Everyone except me. I flipped to a new page in my secret plan book and began to work on my greatest plan yet.

Chapter 3
A New Plan

At recess, I made my way across the playground to The Fortress. The Fortress is our shelter from the noise and chaos of recess. It is a secluded, quiet area where we can discuss ideas without disruption.

Munch and Ralph were still yipping about the talent show.

"Wow!" panted Munch. "A talent show! How cool is that?"

"Zero cool!" wailed Ralph. "Are you crazy? A talent show? Do you remember that book report we had to read out loud in second grade? My parents had to prescribe antianxiety medication for me. Then the medication gave me more anxiety so they had to send me to therapy. Doing stuff in front of people gives me sweaty palms and shortness of breath. And a tingling sensation in my toes. And then I puke."

"Yeah!" cried Munch. "That's a great talent! You could do some stunt puking. You could eat lots of colorful foods and throw up a rainbow. Or throw up through your nose like you did last week when you accidentally thought about spicy sushi. Or you could puke and hit a target. Start practicing now! See if you can hit that kid over there."

"SILENCE!" I commanded. "Number one. Munch, your idea is so repellently **nauseous** that I will not comment on it further. Number two. Please remove your finger from your nose."

Munch pulled his finger out of his nose and inspected it closely. "Does that look a little like a dinosaur to you? This could be my talent!"

"Number three," I continued. "You will not need to develop your own acts for the talent show. You will be helping me with the act that I have already created." I opened my secret book to display my brilliantly rendered plan. "Here is our act."

"Oh boy, Simon. That's your act?" said Mike, swaggering toward The Fortress. "I can hardly wait to see you in the talent show. What are you going to do? Sit on stage and scribble your stupid little plans in your stupid little diary?"

"HA!" laughed Evil Ernie. "A stupid little diary."

"Yeah," said Eviler Ernie. "The diary my grammy

bought me on my birthday is way cooler than yours. It has a lavender cover with a delicate, white lace border around the edges. I wrote a poem about my pet bunny in it."

Mike gaped at Eviler Ernie.

"What?" Ernie whined. "It was a good poem. It's a sonnet called 'Mr. Snuffle-Lumps Is a Soft, Precious Jewel.'"

"We've been over this several times, Ernie," Mike huffed. "If you don't have something mean to say, don't say anything at all."

Eviler Ernie tried again. "My diary is cooler than yours, Simon. It's so cool. It has a little heart-shaped lock on the front. And it even has a key tied to a little satin ribbon. I wear it around my neck so I don't lose it."

Mike buried his face in his hands. "What is WRONG with you?"

Mike and the two Ernies stomped off toward the basketball court, where they liked to hang around and practice teasing people.

Ralph and Munch exploded in laughter.

"Well," I said, "perhaps now we can begin discussing our act in the upcoming talent show." I opened my secret plan book so Munch and Ralph could see my work.

"What is it?" asked Munch, inspecting my brilliantly rendered drawing. "It looks all squiggly like spaghetti. I love spaghetti. Are either of you guys hungry? I'm starving." He pulled a linty wad from his bellybutton, ate it, and then dug for more.

"Want some, Ralph?" he asked.

"Are you crazy?" asked Ralph. "Do you know how unsanitary that is? And anyway, Simon's picture isn't spaghetti. It's obviously a few dozen squirrels dancing on top of a wedding cake shaped like a monster truck driving over a salami and cheese sandwich."

We stared at Ralph.

"Do your parents perform medical experiments on your brain while you sleep?" asked Munch.

"What?" Ralph asked. "Isn't that what it is? It looks like that, especially the wedding cake part. Even though I can't eat wedding cake because of my gluten allergy. And my frosting allergy."

I snapped my book shut.

"Never mind what it looks like," I said. "Although I would like to point out that it looks like neither of the odd and disturbing images that either of you suggested. It looks like the three of us performing in the talent show and winning the grand prize and possibly even becoming the most popular musical group in the world."

"No. It doesn't look like that," said Munch. "Let me see the picture again. Which squiggly thing was supposed to be me?"

"I don't want to be a squiggly thing!" cried Ralph. "Squiggling gives me heart palpitations. Please don't make me squiggle!"

"SILENCE!" I roared. "You will not be squiggling,

Ralph. There is no squiggling involved in my plan at all. It is extremely simple. This plan came to me in an instant when that foul girl showed me the picture of those **insipid** Funkee Boyz."

"You mean her?" asked Munch, pointing at Stacy.

Somehow she had breached The Fortress's defenses and was standing right behind me, befouling the air with a light, fruity scent.

"Hey, guys. What are you doing?" she asked. "I thought I heard you talking about The Funkee Boyz."

I pointed at her. "How did you gain access to The Fortress, foul girl?"

"I just sort of walked over." The foul girl waved her hands around airily. Her glittery, pink nail polish twinkled in the sun. "Your fortress is just a little weed patch at the edge of the playground."

"Number one. It is not just a little weed patch. It is The Fortress. It is *our* fortress; a special place, far from the **turmoil** of the playground, where we have gathered since the days of our youth to discuss matters of great importance. Number two. Your presence here only serves to upset the **robust** air of **machismo** that defines the very atmosphere of The Fortress."

Stacy sniffed, wrinkling up her freckled nose. "It kind of smells like farts."

"Excuse me," Ralph whispered, blushing. "My stomach is a bit upset. My father diagnosed it as chronic **flatulence** and prescribed some gas-reducing pills. I think they made it worse."

Stacy stepped away from Ralph.

"So what are you guys up to?" she asked. "Are you starting a Funkee Boyz fan club? Can I join? I love The Funkee Boyz. I know everything about them."

"We are busy with plans which require nothing from you, foul girl. Be off." I pointed across the playground.

"Oh fine, Simon. You never seem to want my help," Stacy huffed. "But if you need to know anything about The Funkee Boyz, just let me know." She ran off down the hill to play kickball with her friends, leaving behind only the delicate scent of vanilla and oranges.

"Why do you think she's always hanging around, Simon?" asked Ralph.

"I think she likes you," said Munch, bouncing his eyebrows up and down. "I know all about that kind of stuff because the ladies are all crazy about me."

I shook my head. "Ever since the day in first grade when I returned a chocolate chip cookie that Mike and the two Ernies had stolen from her, that foul girl has had a strange fascination with me. She is constantly inquiring about my activities and inflicting her company upon me. I have no time for such nonsense."

"Wait a minute…did she say we're starting a fan club?" asked Ralph. "Can I be the president? Do I get to wear a crown?"

"No. We are not starting a fan club, Ralph. We are starting our own band. We are going to win the talent show and go on to become the most popular musical act in history."

"Uh, Simon?" said Munch, raising his hand. "Just a quick comment.... We don't know how to play any instruments."

I opened my secret plan book and looked over my plan carefully. I seemed to have overlooked that detail.

Chapter 4
Some Stars Are Born, Almost

After recess, I sat at my desk and wondered how I could possibly have overlooked such a critical detail. The fault certainly falls on the foul girl. Her constant interruptions and fruity scent distracted me from my work.

I was deeply engrossed in planning an alternate scheme when Stacy was once again peering over my shoulder.

"Are you making a list of people in the fan club, Simon?" she asked.

"A fan club for Simon?" snorted Mike from his desk. "Who would join a dorky club like that?"

"HA!" laughed Evil Ernie.

"Ha! Ha!" laughed Eviler Ernie. "A Simon fan

club. That's so lame. My fan club that I started for my grammy is much cooler. It's called the My Grammy Is the Best Grammy in the World Club. I'm the president. I'm also the vice president and the secretary and the treasurer. My grammy says it's the coolest club. We have meetings in our family rumpus room every other Tuesday. We have chamomile tea and snack-sized carrot cakes that we bake ourselves. They have cream cheese frosting on them!"

Mike dropped his head to his desk. He banged it gently a few times.

"Oh man, Ernie," he moaned. "You're killing me."

"So what is it, Simon?" asked Stacy. "What are you working on now?"

Mrs. Douglass glanced at the clock and put aside the brochures she was studying. "Okay, class, line up for music."

In general, I dislike music class. I also dislike art and physical education classes. They interfere with my planning time. This morning, however, I realized that music class might be the answer to all my problems.

Throughout the entire lesson, I paid close attention to everything that Mr. Alexander said. I attempted to take notes in my plan book, but very little of the information seemed relevant to forming a band that will win the school talent competition. Most of the instruction seemed to revolve around clapping along with the expression "Ta, ta, tee-tee-ta." I could make nothing of this.

"Well, Simon," said Mr. Alexander, as we lined up at the door after class, "it's good to see that you're finally taking an interest in music."

"Indeed I am, my dear **preceptor** of the musical arts. Over the last few hours I have developed a keen interest in developing my own musical capabilities. In

fact, I wish to enlist your assistance in this **endeavor**."

Mr. Alexander stared at me. "Huh?"

I used to believe that teachers were required to memorize the dictionary before they were allowed to teach. It appears that this is not the case.

"My associates and I wish very much to participate in the upcoming talent show. We would like to start a band and we are somewhat hindered by the fact that we do not know how to play instruments. I would like you to teach me how to play an instrument."

Mr. Alexander looked puzzled. "You mean you want to take lessons?" he asked.

"Yes, I do. I need to be excellent at playing an instrument by Friday. When can we begin?"

Mr. Alexander laughed, though there was nothing **jocular** about my request.

"Are you serious?" asked Mr. Alexander. "You expect to learn how to play an instrument in four days?"

"Of course I do," I answered. "Ralph and Munch are also in the band, so they will require lessons as well."

Mr. Alexander laughed again. "So all three of you need to learn how to play instruments by Friday so you can win the talent show?"

"That is correct," I answered. "So when can we begin?"

"Do you even know which instruments you want to play?" asked Mr. Alexander.

I thought for a moment. "I had not considered that," I admitted. "Are there many to choose from?"

Mr. Alexander sighed. "Hundreds, Simon. Hundreds. And I hate to break it to you, but you can't learn how to play an instrument in just a few days. It takes years and years of practice to become a good musician."

"But that is unacceptable. I do not have years and years. The talent show is Friday and I must win the grand prize."

"You'd better get busy, then," said Mr. Alexander as he ushered me out the door. "Good luck. You're going to need it."

"I will get busy," I told him. "And when my associates and I have claimed the fantastic grand prize at the talent show and rocketed to stardom, do not expect us to name you as an early influence."

"I think I can live with the disappointment," said Mr. Alexander, closing his door.

Back in the classroom I whispered to Ralph and Munch, "We will **convene** at my **domicile** after our daily **internment** has drawn to a conclusion."

Munch and Ralph stared at me. "Huh?"

I sighed. "Meet me at my house after school today."

Chapter 5
After-School Snack

When I arrived at my home after school, my hideous sister, Victoria, was already on the telephone. There are only three activities she regularly engages in: talking on the telephone with her hideous friends; looking at her hideous face in the mirror; and reading fashion magazines to learn how to make herself even more hideous. Not that she requires help with that.

I have often suggested that her time would be better spent reading a dictionary and improving her mind. It is obvious that she is never going to improve her face.

Victoria sneered and stuck her tongue out at me as I walked into the kitchen. I ignored her and sat at the table to begin my planning.

My mother walked into the kitchen holding my brother, Simon 2.0. I have been training him as my apprentice since he was born. I will teach him to be just like me, and together we shall overthrow Victoria.

My mother placed Simon 2.0 on the floor next to Fido's food dish. Fido is the vicious attack dog that I have also been training to help us in our battle against Victoria the Hideous.

"Hello, Simon, honey. How was your day?" my mother asked.

"Number one. Do not call me 'honey.' Number two. My day was much like every other day at school—unvaried **monotony**—with one exception. It appears that the school is sponsoring a talent show and offering extraordinary prizes for the winners."

"Cheese!" squealed Simon 2.0.

Despite all the hard work I have done to build his vocabulary, almost all the words my brother says are food words.

"Well, that's nice, honey," my mother said. "So what are you planning to do in the show?"

"Again, I beg you; do not call me 'honey.' As for my talent, I am putting together a band with Ralph and Munch. We shall win the special prize offered at the talent show and then rise to stardom in much the same way as The Funkee Boyz."

Victoria cackled and snorted into the phone. "Oh my gosh. You'll never guess what my doofus little brother just said. He said he's going to start a band with his disgusting friends.... Oh, I know. He wants to be like The Funkee Boyz. As if a little doofus like him could ever be even close to cool."

I pointed at Victoria. "Fido! Attack!"

Fido merely sat in the corner, licking his fur.

"Oh, puh-leeeeze," Victoria said into the phone. "Now he's trying to get his cat to attack me.... Oh, I know. He's a total doofus. He named his cat 'Fido' so now he says it's a dog."

I am fully aware that Fido is a cat. Fido is not aware that he is a cat, however. Since the day we brought him home from the shelter, I have been training him to be a terrifying attack dog.

As an attack dog, Fido has proved to be somewhat disappointing.

I tried again. "Fido! Destroy this menace to society!"

Fido looked up, hacked up a hairball, and continued grooming himself.

"Pudding!" squealed my brother, picking up the hairball and squeezing it tightly in his fist.

"OH, EEEEWWWWW! I'll call you back!" shrieked Victoria, hanging up the phone.

Simon 2.0 toddled toward Victoria, waving the hairball out in front of him.

"Yes!" I cried. "Wipe it on her hideous pants!"

Victoria leapt away from him. "NO! Mom, help!"

"Smear it on her, Simon 2.0," I cheered.

Mother intercepted my brother and carried him to the sink to wash off his hand. "That's not pudding, sweetie.

And Simon, his name is Spencer, not Simon 2.0. How many times do I have to explain this to you? He's going to get confused if we all call him different names."

"Then let us all refer to him as Simon 2.0 until I am able to upgrade him. Then we shall refer to him as Simon 2.1."

"And we shall refer to you as 'Doofus,'" sneered Victoria as she stalked out of the room.

Mother washed off the hairball and returned Simon 2.0 to the floor. "So what kind of music are you and your friends going to play, Simon?"

"We have yet to decide that," I explained. "Munch and Ralph will be arriving any moment now and there is still much planning to which I must attend. If you will excuse me." I opened my plan book and returned to my work.

"All right, honey," Mother said as she led Simon 2.0 into the living room. "But don't be too loud when you're practicing. We don't want to disturb Mrs. Annand."

Last week a strange, wrinkled old woman moved into the house next door. I have seen her only once since her arrival. She peered out her window at me as I trained Fido to attack a life-sized drawing of Victoria that I had created. When I noticed her watching, her curtains snapped shut. I have not seen her since.

I was hard at work on my plan for winning the talent show when Ralph and Munch marched through the kitchen door.

Munch picked up Fido's hairball from the side of the sink. "All right! Pudding!"

Chapter 6
Meet Mrs. Annand

Munch was wiping at his mouth as we walked out into my backyard.

"Jeez, Simon, I can't believe you let me eat that hairball," he moaned.

"Oohhhh, please don't even talk about it," groaned Ralph. "I haven't seen you do anything that disgusting since lunch. Why did you eat a hairball?"

"I thought it was pudding," said Munch.

"You thought that a hairy, wet blob sitting on the counter next to the sink looked like pudding?" I asked.

"Yeah," admitted Munch. "I thought it was one of your Aunt Fluffy's treats."

My Aunt Fluffy frequently watches my younger

brother when my parents are out of the house. She makes **noxious concoctions** of wheat germ, tofu, carob, soy milk, and alfalfa sprouts and then claims that they taste exactly like chocolate chip cookies.

"Now that you mention it," I said, "I can see how you might confuse a squashed-up hairball with my Aunt Fluffy's wheat gluten pudding with vegetable-based non-dairy whipped topping and granola sprinkles. They do look similar."

"They actually taste similar, too," said Munch, smacking his lips. "But the hairball was a little more zesty, with a delicate hint of fish and a robust, peppery finish."

Ralph turned slightly green. A thin sheen of sweat broke out across his upper lip. "Please..." he whimpered. "Stop talking about it...."

"Kind of like school-lunch taco meat," continued Munch.

Ralph wobbled back and forth. "Oohhhhhh...."

"We are not here to discuss Munch's **unpalatable** food choices," I said. "We are here to form our new band so we can win one of the fantastic prizes being offered at the talent show."

"What are the prizes?" asked Munch. "I hope it's a...ooooh! Look! A snack!" Munch picked a small white glob from the grass and tossed it into his mouth. He chewed for a minute, frowned, and looked up into the tree branches. "Do lots of birds perch up there?"

Ralph gagged. "I hope the prize is a new toothbrush for you. I'm never letting you use mine again."

"I only used it once!" Munch cried. "I had to get the taste of your mom's cookie out of my mouth."

"I keep telling you that wasn't a cookie!" Ralph said. "It was a bar of allergy-free oatmeal soap!"

"SILENCE!" I roared. "We are discussing the prizes offered at the talent show. I have heard of similar competitions on television and it is not uncommon for the prizes to be hundreds of thousands of dollars. Everyone knows how much money schools have. That is why all teachers are so rich. I am certain we can expect that the top prize will be at least a half million dollars. Perhaps more."

"Whoa..." whispered Munch and Ralph together.

"You could buy your very own toothbrush to have at my house," Ralph told Munch.

"And you could buy some cookies that don't taste like soap," Munch said.

"So now, perhaps you see why I am so eager to begin practicing," I continued. "What have you brought for instruments?"

"I looked all through my little sisters' toy box, but I couldn't find much," said Munch, taking a few items out of his backpack. "I have a kazoo and this rubber band guitar I made out of a tissue box in kindergarten."

"Cool!" said Ralph. "I remember making those guitars in Miss Debbie's class! That was the time you ate all that paste and my mom had to pump your stomach."

"Yeah," said Munch. "That paste was great. Did you know that Miss Debbie only uses non-toxic paste now because of me? It's too bad. That original toxic stuff actually had a nice wintergreen sort of flavor, layered with balanced notes of spearmint and citrus."

I sighed. "Evidently, even the lure of a half million dollars is not enough to prevent the two of you from discussing your **odious gustatory** adventures. I would like to remind you, once again, that the prize will be hundreds of thousands of dollars, as well as worldwide fame. Can we continue with the rehearsal, please? Ralph, what instruments were you able to gather?"

"Umm..." Ralph shuffled his feet a bit. "Actually, blowing into instruments kind of makes me woozy and dizzy. Plus, I have chapped lips. I thought that maybe I could clap. But softly, because I have very sensitive skin."

"You can borrow my sister's kazoo," said Munch, holding out the filthy, chewed-up instrument.

Ralph backed away from it. "Uhhh, I don't think so. It doesn't look too...um...clean. Anyway, I just said that blowing into things makes me woozy."

I held up a hand. "I expected such a complication, Ralph, and I am prepared for it." I pointed to the picnic table, where I had lined up four empty yogurt containers next to two spoons.

Ralph's eyes bugged in horror. "Simon! You know I'm lactose intolerant!"

"Of course I am aware of that, Ralph. These containers are empty. You can use the spoons to strike the upended containers. The subsequent **concussive**

reverberation will provide the rhythmic beats necessary for our musical compositions."

"Huh?" said Ralph and Munch.

"You can hit them like drums," I explained.

"Oh," said Ralph.

"So we have guitar and drums now," said Munch. "What are you going to play, Simon?"

"I am glad you asked, Munch," I said, opening my secret plan book. "I have written the words to our first hit song and I shall be singing."

"Cool!" said Ralph and Munch. "What's the song called?"

I cleared my throat. "The song is called 'My Sister Victoria Is a Hideous She-Beast.' I think we should begin playing the song."

Munch tried to tune his guitar, but managed only to snap one of the rubber bands off, shooting it into Ralph's eye.

"OW! MY EYE!" yelped Ralph.

"Too bad your parents aren't eye doctors," laughed Munch.

"SILENCE!" I commanded. "We have much to accomplish this afternoon."

I counted off the song, as I have heard musicians do, and we all began playing.

"One, two, three, four..."

"Victoria is my repellent, ugly sister,
When she went away nobody missed her.

When she returned everyone was sad
Because her personality is so bad."

Ralph and Munch joined in and played as I sang.

"My sister is a hideous she-beast.
My parents like her the least.
From a zoo, it seems, she was released,
Oh she is no beauty, just a beast."

Ralph played louder, so Munch played louder, so I naturally had to sing louder. So Ralph played even louder, so Munch played even louder, so I sang even louder. We were playing so loudly, we never heard the window of the house next door being thrown open. We never heard Mrs. Annand shrieking and yelling at us. We never heard the super-dry, rock-hard, fat-free, high-fiber bran muffin whistling through the air toward us.

It bounced off Munch's head and rolled to a stop in the dirt at our feet. We all stopped playing and stared at the muffin.

Then the screeching started. "What is that horrible noise?"

Mrs. Annand's wrinkled prune head poked out her window. "What's going on out there? It sounds like a few dozen squirrels dancing on top of a wedding cake shaped like a monster truck driving over a salami and cheese sandwich. I'm trying to watch my programs

here! How am I supposed to watch the TV with you making that horrible noise?"

Munch rubbed his head where the muffin had hit him. "Owwwww," he moaned.

"And stop that moaning!" yelled Mrs. Annand.

I strode toward the dreadful, shrieking woman. "We are practicing for a show—" I began.

"I don't care what kind of sick, squirrel dancing,

monster truck, salami and cheese show you think you're practicing for, I'm trying to watch my stories on the TV! I want it QUIET! I also want my muffin back. I'm saving it for a special occasion."

We all looked at the muffin sitting in the dirt at our feet.

Munch picked it up and handed it to Mrs. Annand through her window, which promptly slammed shut.

Munch trudged back across the yard.

The window shot open again and the super-dry, rock-hard, fat-free, high-fiber bran muffin flew out and hit Munch in the back of the head. "AND STOP ALL THAT TRUDGING!" screeched Mrs. Annand. "And give me back my muffin. I'm saving that for a special occasion."

Munch once again handed the muffin back to Mrs. Annand and tiptoed back across the yard.

Munch rubbed his head. "I don't think this is going to work," he said.

Chapter 7
Another New Plan

At dinner that night, I was still furious. "This is an outrage! That horrid, shrieking woman next door has ruined my plan. How can we practice for the talent show if she is constantly bombarding us with projectile muffins and howling at us?"

"I'll bet her howling sounded better than your music," snorted Victoria.

"Muffins!" squealed Spencer.

"Projectile muffins?" asked my father. "What are you talking about, Simon?"

My father is an editor for a literary magazine. He should understand what the words "projectile muffins" mean.

"I'm talking about that **diabolical** woman's **propensity** for catapulting muffins at us as we attempt to rehearse our songs."

Father looked at Mother for help. "What is he talking about?" he asked.

Mother sighed. "It seems that Simon had a bit of a problem with Mrs. Annand."

"I see...," said Father.

"Simon, honey," said Mother, "You and your friends need to find a game to play that isn't going to disturb that sweet lady."

"Number one. Do not call me 'honey.' Number two. My associates and I are not playing a game. We are rehearsing for the talent show in an effort to win a fabulous prize and become musical **icons**. Number three. Mrs. Annand is not a sweet lady. She is a dangerous muffin-launching lunatic."

"So what sort of act have you guys come up with for the talent show?" Father asked.

"We will be performing an original musical number in the style of The Funkee Boyz," I answered.

Victoria burst out laughing—a horrible, cackling noise like a chicken laying a fifty-pound egg. "I can't believe that a doofus like you thinks he can be anything like The Funkee Boyz."

Once again, Father looked at Mother for help. "The funky boys?" he asked.

Mother shrugged.

Victoria sighed and rolled her eyes. "The *Funkee*

Boyz are, like, the coolest band in the whole world, Dad. Everybody knows that."

"Ahhh, yes. Of course," said Father. "How silly of me to have forgotten." He turned to me. "I know that you and your friends need to practice, Simon, but you also need to remember that your practice shouldn't disturb other people. You have to treat people the same way they treat you."

I was about to explain to my father that he should be lecturing Mrs. Annand on how to behave like a human, when I realized that he was right.

"Father," I said, "You are absolutely correct. Dear, sweet, kindhearted Mrs. Annand deserves to be treated the same way that she has treated my associates and me."

After dinner, I excused myself from the table and spent the rest of the evening devising a new plan.

Chapter 8
Counter-Attacks and Pretty Spotted Ponies

The next day at recess, I met Munch and Ralph in The Fortress.

"Gentlemen," I announced, "We are now one day closer to the talent show and we have still not perfected our act."

"Yeah. Because of that crazy old lady," said Munch. "My head still hurts. Ralph's mother said I might have a concussion. What do you think that old lady does with those muffins? You don't seriously think she eats them, do you?"

I shook my head. "Munch, my good man, I have no idea how that **maniacal** old crone employs her muffins. My only concern now is that we be able to continue rehearsing so we can win the prize."

"Well, we can't practice at my house," said Ralph. "My parents only allow classical music. Anything else drives them crazy."

"And I don't think we can practice at my house, either," said Munch. "My mother is at work after school. I can't have anyone over when she's not home. That's why I usually hang out at Ralph's place in the afternoons, even though I have to listen to all that classical music. That stuff drives me crazy. Plus, the snacks at his house are awful. Did I ever tell you about—"

"SILENCE!" I commanded. "Do you really believe that I will allow myself to be driven out of my own home by that **geriatric barbarian**? I will not bow down to her demands. She will not deny me the basic human right of practicing for the talent show without being bombarded by bran muffins."

"Bran muffins give me a stomachache," said Ralph.

"They give me a headache," said Munch.

I climbed to the top of a rock in the corner of The Fortress and continued my inspirational speech. "I have a dream! I have a dream that today, even the yard next to Mrs. Annand, a yard sweltering with dangerous muffin missiles, will be transformed into an oasis of freedom and justice and musical delight."

Ralph raised his hand. "Um, excuse me, Simon?

Are you saying that you're still planning to practice in your yard? Even after what happened yesterday?"

"Are you nuts?" asked Munch.

I looked down at them. "Oh yes. We shall practice in my yard today. I have a plan and after today we shall be free at last, free at last, free from her muffins, free at last!"

I stepped down from the rock and pulled out my secret plan book.

"Look at this," I said.

"Oh, Simon! Do you have something to show us? Some new secret plan in your stupid little diary?" Mike McAlpine and the two Ernies swaggered into The Fortress.

I have no idea why these three buffoons seem to derive such joy from tormenting us. I suspect that it all stems from the time I returned the foul girl's snack to her in first grade. They seek revenge, I suppose.

"We have no time for your nonsense today, Michael," I said. "You and your dim-witted goons should wander off and find a hole to fall in."

Mike looked shocked. He turned to the two Ernies. "Did you hear what he just said to us?"

"Yeah," said Evil Ernie.

"Uhhh, not really," said Eviler Ernie. "I was thinking about ponies. My grammy said she's taking me on a pony ride after school today. I get to pick out whichever pony I want! I hope they have a spotted chestnut

pony. I'd really like to ride a spotted chestnut pony. I think I'd look grand."

Mike and Evil Ernie gaped at Eviler Ernie.

"*Grand?*" mocked Mike, "You'd look *grand?* Who talks like that? Seriously, Ernie, we've got a lot of work to do with you. Come on."

Mike hurried off toward the basketball courts, followed closely by the two Ernies.

"I'll bet ponies make you puke," said Munch, pointing at Ralph.

"Actually," said Ralph, "ponies do not make me puke. The *idea* of ponies makes me a little queasy, but real, actual ponies give me a dry, hacking cough."

I held up my secret plan book and tapped an open page. "Do you remember why we are here?" I asked.

Ralph and Munch stared at the picture.

"Is that another picture of fireworks at a spaghetti factory?" asked Munch.

Ralph snorted and pointed to my drawing. "No way, Munch. That's obviously a hamster with a mohawk juggling meatballs in a giant pot of corn chowder."

Munch gaped at Ralph. "Are your parents testing new medications on you or something?" he asked.

"What?" cried Ralph. "Isn't that what it is?"

I tapped on my plan book once again. "This, in fact, is my plan for retaliating against Mrs. Annand. It was my father who suggested the plan to me. He suggested that we should treat Mrs. Annand as kindly as she has treated us. With that in mind, I have devised my most clever scheme to date. If Mrs. Annand sees fit to hurl her muffins at us today, we shall be ready with a counterattack."

Before Ralph and Munch could ask any questions, the bell rang. I snapped my secret plan book shut and we all lined up for class.

Chapter 9
Snack Time!

I raced home after school and was greeted at the door by my Aunt Fluffy.

"Hello, my little Sweetie-Poops!" she squealed, throwing the door open wide. "How was your day at school?"

I glared at her. Evidently I still need to work on my glare. She did not burst into flames, but I did smell smoke.

"Number one. Do not ever call me 'Sweetie-Poops.' I have told you this many times. Number two. My day was the usual mix of **tedium** and **ennui**. Number three. My associates are arriving shortly and shall no doubt be in dire need of nourishment. How have you exercised your **morbid culinary** talents today?"

Aunt Fluffy stared at me. "Huh?"

Perhaps she would understand me if she spent more time reading the dictionary and less time looking through cookbooks for the criminally insane.

"Food," I explained. "My friends are coming over and they will want food. What unspeakable health-food horrors have you created today?"

"Food? You want food? MY food? Oh, I'm so excited to share this latest creation with you!" she crowed. "Oh, Simon, Sweetie-Poops, you are simply going to love this. Come on." She grabbed my arm and yanked me toward the kitchen.

"Unhand me this minute," I demanded, shaking my arm free. "I will follow of my own **volition**." I followed her to the kitchen where thick, foul-smelling smoke billowed from a pot on the stove.

So, the smoke I smelled earlier was not from my glaring powers.

That was a disappointment.

A horrid stench filled the entire kitchen, as if a filthy sock had been stuffed with rancid tuna fish and left to ripen in the sun for a few months. Simon 2.0 sat on the floor playing with a fire truck, pretending that the stove was a burning building.

"Barbecue!" he squealed.

This seemed like an excellent opportunity to help Simon 2.0 develop his vocabulary skills. I pointed to the pot and said, "Can you say '**coagulated** clot of compost'?"

"Compost!" he squealed.

"That is close enough, I suppose. Excellent work!" I patted his head.

"Oh dear," mumbled Aunt Fluffy, waving away some of the smoke and peering into the pot. "It's almost done!" she chirped.

I smiled. Aunt Fluffy's treats were an important part of my plan for this afternoon.

Aunt Fluffy waved away more of the smoke and picked up a large wooden spoon.

"Fire!" Spencer said.

"No, no, sweetie," said Aunt Fluffy, waving away even more smoke. "It's fine. It always smokes like this."

I took my secret plan book to the fresh air of the front steps and waited for Munch and Ralph. It was not long before they arrived, creeping cautiously up the walk, looking anxiously from side to side.

"Is it safe?" whispered Munch.

"What are you talking about?" I asked.

Munch and Ralph cringed and shushed me. "Is *she* home?" hissed Ralph, pointing toward Mrs. Annand's house.

"I certainly hope Mrs. Annand is home," I announced boldly, "because today she will have a taste of her own medicine."

"Medicine?" asked Munch. "Is she sick?"

"I could get my parents to take a look at her," said

Ralph, "but I don't want to see her if she's sick. Sick people give me a low-grade fever. So does medicine, actually."

"Medicine gives you a fever?" asked Munch.

"Well, yeah. Just a low-grade one, though."

I find Munch and Ralph to be irritating at times.

This was one of those times.

"My neighbor is neither sick nor in need of medicine. What I was attempting to **convey** is that today we shall be able to practice in peace. I have a plan. Follow me."

"This plan isn't going to wind up like your last plan, is it, Simon?" Munch asked.

"Oh, I hope not," Ralph groaned. "My parents are going to be furious if they have to replace any more windows. Or front doors. Or chimneys. Or car tires."

"That was an unfortunate miscalculation that could have happened to anyone," I sighed. "This plan is far superior to any of my previous plans."

I opened the door to the kitchen and our noses were assaulted by the stinging odor of Aunt Fluffy's **mephitic** dessert.

"Oh boy! Snacks!" yelped Munch.

"Oh no. Snacks," moaned Ralph.

Aunt Fluffy looked up from the pot she was stirring. "Hello, boys!" she chirped. "Come on in. I've just finished cooking this."

She lifted the spoon out of the pot. It was covered

with a glistening, **gelatinous** paste that trembled and jiggled as she waved the spoon around.

Munch's eyes grew wide. "Is that honey-sweetened bean-curd raisin pudding with ginger-glazed carrots?" he asked.

Aunt Fluffy's face lit up. "Yes, it is!" she sang. "And I put in extra bean curd and a handful of soy protein granules! Grab some bowls from the cupboard there."

The horrid brown goo quivered and shimmered on the spoon.

"Whoopee!" yelled Munch, running to the cupboard to grab a bowl. "Fill 'er up! Ralph's parents tried to feed me unsalted, gluten-free, reduced-flavor crackers today!"

Ralph stared at the hideous glop and all the color drained out of his face.

I led Ralph to the cupboard and handed him a large bowl. "Take it," I whispered, shoving the bowl into Ralph's hands. "It is all part of my plan."

I nudged Ralph gently toward Aunt Fluffy. She smiled broadly as she plopped the horrible, steaming mess into Ralph's bowl.

Ralph started to sweat and whimper.

"Could Ralph please have an extra helping?" I asked.

"Of course he can," answered Aunt Fluffy sweetly. "There you go, honey." She dropped another wet pile of pudding into Ralph's bowl.

Ralph's eyes glazed over and his lower lip quivered. Aunt Fluffy filled my bowl, and Ralph and I went out the back door to join Munch.

Once we were out in the backyard, Ralph spun around and said, "What did you do that for, Simon? Why did you ask for an extra serving? You know I can't eat honey-sweetened bean-curd raisin pudding with ginger-glazed carrots because of my irritable bowel syndrome."

"Why, of course I do, my weak-stomached friend," I replied, patting Ralph's arm. "I asked for the extra serving because I knew we would need it." I pointed to the picnic table where Munch sat, licking his already emptied bowl.

"You mean you don't expect me to eat this?" Ralph asked.

"Of course not," I answered. "I expect you to throw it."

Chapter 10
Sharing the Kindness, Feeling the Love

"We need to practice for the upcoming talent show," I explained. "Mrs. Annand is preventing us from practicing by hurling her deadly baked goods at us. She has shared her snacks with us, now it is time for us to return the favor. When she throws her life-threatening muffin at us today, we will throw back my Aunt Fluffy's pudding."

Ralph and Munch looked shocked.

"You really expect us to throw pudding at an old lady?" asked Ralph.

"And waste good food?" added Munch.

Over the years, I have found that Munch and Ralph are occasionally slow to grasp my plans; but once they

understand them, they are generally eager to participate in them.

Not this time, however.

"Yes and no," I explained. "*Yes*, I do expect you to
throw pudding. And *no*, I do not expect you to waste
good food. Number one. You will be putting it to good
use, not wasting it. Number two. It is not good. To be
honest, I am not even certain that this pudding can be
classified as food. Now, let us begin our rehearsal."

"What if she starts throwing muffins again?" whined
Munch. "My head still really hurts from yesterday.
Ralph's mother thinks I should have my head examined."

"Actually, she says that all the time," said Ralph.
"It's not just about the muffin yesterday."

I thought for a moment. As much as I did not wish
to wait any longer before putting my plan into action,
it seemed wise to take a few basic precautions.

"Yes," I said, "I suppose some safety equipment is
essential until the muffin threat is completely elimi-
nated. Let us see what we can find."

I led Ralph and Munch through the house and
garage. We gathered everything we needed for pro-
tection, got ourselves geared up for battle, and were
soon ready to begin rehearsal.

I pointed to the picnic table. "Ralph, your drums
await you over there. Munch, did you bring your guitar today?"

"Well, yeah, I brought it, but..." Munch shrugged
his shoulders.

"But what?" I asked, irritably. I was not in the mood to hear about delays to my plan.

"Well…I guess it didn't age too well. I think the rubber band strings are kind of old and dried up." He pulled the guitar out of his backpack. "They keep snapping and flying off. There's only one string left."

I eyed the guitar. "How many strings are you able to play at once?" I asked.

Munch thought. "Um. One, I guess."

"Then there is no problem, is there?"

I continued. "All that remains is to place ourselves around the yard so that we can return fire when Mrs. Annand begins launching baked goods. Ralph, I will place a large bowl of Aunt Fluffy's pudding here on the table, next to your drums. Munch, you will stand here underneath the tree to draw her fire."

"Draw her fire?" asked Munch. "What does that mean?"

"It means that you will act as a target. While Mrs. Annand is discharging her ammunition at you, Ralph and I will hurl the pudding at her."

Munch's eyes grew wide. "You mean I'm going to get hit with one of those muffins again? On purpose? Are you nuts? I think she gave me brain damage yesterday."

I sighed. "I will not speculate on the condition of your brain, Munch, but today you will be safe. You are securely shielded by the latest in high-tech anti-muffin protective gear. And I do not expect you to simply sit there and get hit with a muffin. You merely need to draw her fire, then, as soon as she throws, you can jump behind the tree to safety."

Munch did not look convinced. "And where will you be?" he asked me.

I smiled. "That is the genius of my plan. I will be up in the tree, hidden from view and ready to unleash pudding-fueled fury upon Mrs. Annand."

"Why do you get to go up in the tree, hidden from view?" asked Munch.

"Yeah," said Ralph, "Munch and I are easy targets down here."

I did not appreciate the tone of their comments. "My dear associates," I explained, "I am the only member of the band who does not need to hold an instrument. How could you sit in the tree, play your instrument, and launch pudding? It simply is not possible."

"Well, I guess you have a point," said Munch.

"Yeah," agreed Ralph, "I guess. But how come I can't sing and you play the drums?"

"You do not know the words," I answered. "Now let us begin."

I picked up my bowl of pudding and handed it to Munch.

"Oh, boy! Yum! Thanks," said Munch.

"Do not even consider eating that. You will hand it to me once I am in position."

Munch frowned. "I can't believe we're going to waste all this delicious pudding."

I hoisted myself up into the tree. "When we win the talent show, you can use your share of the prize money to buy all the pudding you want. Now hand the bowl to me."

Soon we were all in place and ready to begin.

"Remember," I said, "the prize is at least a half a million dollars. Put some feeling into it."

I counted off the song.

"One...two...three...four...

"Well, my sister is a creepy freak,
She has a nose just like a beak.

"Anyone who sees her face
Runs to find a hiding place.

"My sister, my sister, the freak.
My sister, my sister, the freak."

Ralph tapped tentatively on the yogurt containers, producing a sickly, hollow sound. Munch whipped his head back and forth and windmilled his arm violently against the one remaining string of his guitar. Despite all his impressive-looking effort, he managed to produce only the faintest twanging sound.

"She looks just like an ugly toad
That got run over in the road.

"I think she does not have a brain
She is dumber than a coffee stain.

"My sister, my sis—"

Just as our song was beginning to come together, Mrs. Annand's window flew open. Her angry, pinched face popped out.

"What is that horrible noise?" she shrieked. She raised her spotty, claw-like hand to throw a muffin.

This was our moment of glory. Our moment to shine. We would show everyone that we could overcome any obstacle on our quest to become the most popular musical group the world has ever known.

But instead of shining, Munch panicked and held his guitar up as a shield. The last rubber band string snapped and flew into the air just as I yelled "FIRE!"

The rubber band hit me in the eye as I reared back to throw my bowl of pudding. I cried out in pain and lost my balance. Teetering back and forth on the branch, I grabbed for the trunk of the tree to balance myself, but the bowl dropped from my hands, splashing pudding all over the branch where I stood. The bowl spun through the air and bounced off Munch's head.

"AAAHHHH!" Munch screamed. "I've got honey-sweetened bean-curd raisin pudding with ginger-glazed carrots up my nose!!"

Munch staggered toward the picnic table and tripped. He grabbed at the air and knocked Ralph's bowl of pudding into Ralph's face.

"AAAAHHHH!" screamed Ralph. "I've got pudding all over my sensitive skin! IT BURNS!"

Ralph stumbled across the yard, wiping at the pudding in his eyes. He tripped and landed on top of Munch. Both of them toppled to the ground at the foot of the tree just as I slipped on the pudding, plummeted from the branch, and crashed down on top of them.

The momentary silence was broken by the whizzing sound of a super-dry, rock-hard, fat-free, high-fiber bran muffin rocketing through the air.

"Ouch!" cried Munch, as the muffin bounced off his head.

Then the shrieking started again.

"What is that horrible noise?!? What kind of shenanigans are you rowdy hoodlums up to this time? I'm trying to watch my stories on the TV and all I can hear is the terrible ruckus you're making."

We moaned and tried to untangle ourselves from each other.

"And stop all that moaning!" yelled Mrs. Annand.

Munch stood up and wiped the pudding from his face.

"And give me back that muffin," demanded Mrs. Annand. "I'm saving it for a special occasion."

Munch bent down and picked up the muffin. He

lurched over to Mrs. Annand's window and handed it to her.

She eyed him suspiciously. "What is all this tom-foolery? What's the matter with you children these days? All that rock and roll music you're playing must have given you the brain damage."

"Actually," said Munch, "I think your muffin gave me brain damage."

"Nonsense!" snapped Mrs. Annand, slamming her window shut.

Munch turned and staggered back toward Ralph and me, licking at the pudding still splashed across his face.

I took out my secret plan book and opened it to the next page. "It is time for a new plan."

Chapter 11
Outside Opinions

We wiped pudding off ourselves as we walked to the front steps.

"Oh man," moaned Munch. "I got about a gallon of that pudding up my nose. I think those ginger-glazed carrots are crammed up in my sinuses. And you were wrong, Simon. We did waste the pudding. We never even hit Mrs. Annand with it."

"And," cried Ralph, "I got pudding in my eye. It's probably going to give me pink eye!"

"Actually," said Munch, "It will probably give you pudding eye, which is even worse than pink eye."

"Oh no," moaned Ralph. "Worse than pink eye?"

"Way worse than pink eye," said Munch, "because

when you get pudding eye, your eye gets all filled up with..." Munch stopped talking and wrinkled up his face. He held up a finger. "Excuse me for a minute," he said. He placed his finger against one nostril and blew a large piece of ginger-glazed carrot out the other. "Aaahhh, that's better," he said. He picked up the carrot and popped it into his mouth.

"Eeeeuuuugghh!!" wailed Ralph. He clutched his stomach and leaned over the side of the stairs. "I can't believe you ate that!"

"SILENCE!!" I commanded.

"Yeah! Silence! The Chief Dork of the Dork Patrol is about to speak!"

Mike and the two Ernies were standing on the sidewalk in front of the house. Munch picked another carrot from his nose and inspected it.

"Oh, nasty!" yelled Mike.

"Yeah, nasty," said Evil Ernie.

"Totally nasty!" agreed Eviler Ernie.

Mike smiled at Eviler Ernie. "Good," he said. "Now you're getting the hang of it. That wasn't so hard, was it, buddy?"

Eviler Ernie smiled and blushed.

Munch ate the carrot. "What are you guys doing standing in the road spying on us? You need to steal ideas for the talent show because your act is so lame?"

"No way, dork," said Mike. "Our act is going to be amazing."

"Yeah," said Evil Ernie.

"Yeah," said Eviler Ernie. "And we weren't spying on you. We were passing by on the way to my grammy's house for our weekly knitting lesson. This week we're learning the butterfly stitch."

"ERNIE!!" shrieked Mike. He grabbed Eviler Ernie by the shoulders and hissed something into his ear. Eviler Ernie slumped and scowled.

Then Mike turned back to us. "Why are you dorks dressed up like that? Did you go to a dork costume party?"

"Oooh!" squealed Eviler Ernie. "One time, I went to a costume party with—"

Mike held up a finger and silenced Ernie. "Remember what I just said, Ernie?"

Ernie crossed his arms and dropped his head to his chest.

"Not that I see how our activities are any of your business, Michael, but we are preparing our act for the talent show," I said. "We are going to win the fabulous first prize."

"HA!" laughed Mike.

"HA!" laughed Evil Ernie.

"HO!" laughed Eviler Ernie.

Mike turned and looked at him. "No, Ernie. Not 'HO!' It's 'HA!' Try again."

"HA!" laughed Eviler Ernie.

"Good," said Mike, patting Ernie on the shoulder.

Mike turned back to me. "You don't have a chance of winning. I'm going to win the first prize with my amazing magic act." He pointed to the two Ernies. "And these guys are my assistants."

I sighed. "Michael, there is no way that your feeble attempts at **conjuring** and **prestidigitation** can compete with our show-stopping musical performance."

Mike and the two Ernies stared at me.

"Huh?" they all said together.

"He said that we're going to beat you," explained Ralph.

I was proud of Ralph. "Excellent job," I said, patting him on the shoulder.

"HA!" laughed Mike.

"HA! HA!" laughed Evil Ernie.

"HA! HA! HA! HA! HA! HA! HA! HA! HA! HA! HA! HA! HA! HA! HA! HA! HA! HA! HA! HA! HA! HA! HA! HA! HA! HA! HA! HA! HA! HA! HA!" laughed Eviler Ernie.

"Don't overdo it, Ernie," said Mike.

"Sorry," mumbled Eviler Ernie.

"It's okay," said Mike. "You're doing a great job, champ. I'm really proud of you." Then he turned back to me. "And how do you think you're going to win, dork? By covering yourself in brown slime and dressing up like freaks?"

"We're dressed up in the latest in high-tech anti-muffin protective gear, Mike," sneered Munch.

"Anti-muffin gear?" mocked Mike. "To protect you from scary muffins?"

"Scary muffins," sneered Evil Ernie.

"I love muffins!" said Eviler Ernie. "My grammy makes delicious lemon poppy-seed muffins sometimes. If I'm at her house, she lets me help her bake them. I get to wear an apron and measure out the sugar and sift the flour. Then, while they're baking, we play cribbage or walk around in her herb garden and build fairy houses."

Mike grabbed his head with both hands and moaned. "Oh man, Ernie. You were doing so well." He grabbed Ernie's arm and pulled him down the street. Evil Ernie trotted along behind them.

"I like that trick!" called Munch. "The disappearing Mike and Ernies trick!"

"Have fun knitting!" Ralph sang out.

Mike turned around and growled at us. "Don't even bother rehearsing your dork band routine anymore, because we're going to win that talent show."

"Yeah!" said Evil Ernie.

"Yeah!" said Eviler Ernie. "We're going to win! Unless you win. Then we won't win."

Mike shook his head.

"But we WILL win!" Eviler Ernie yelled.

Chapter 12
More Outside Opinions

"Well," I said as we watched them round the corner, "it is always a refreshing treat when Michael and his **cretinous** companions stop by for a little visit, but now we have more pressing matters that require our attention."

"Yeah. Like getting this pudding out of my eye," said Ralph. "I think it's getting infected."

"And getting these ginger-glazed carrots out of my nose," said Munch, blowing out another one. "They hurt like crazy, but they are delicious! They have a bold, earthy flavor with satisfying, sharp accents."

"I was referring to our musical act," I said. "We need to rehearse if we are going to win that prize. We need a new location where we can practice without the constant threat of being hit by airborne pastries."

"We need more than a new place to rehearse," said Munch.

"What else do we require?" I asked.

"Instruments," said Munch, holding his smashed guitar out to me. "My whole guitar got smashed when you fell out of the tree and landed on me. "

I took it from him and inspected the sad, crumpled remains.

"This certainly introduces an additional challenge to our quest for domination of the music industry."

"Hi, guys! What's that in your hand, Simon?"

Stacy was standing on the sidewalk pointing at the guitar and looking us over with eyes as brown as hot fudge. It seemed that the entire population of our town was working together to prevent us from winning the talent show.

"It's my guitar," said Munch. "Well, it was

my guitar before Simon fell out of a tree and crushed it."

"You fell out of a tree, Simon? Are you okay?" She moved in my direction.

"Come no closer, foul girl!" I ordered, holding up my hand. "My health and personal well-being are no concerns of yours."

She stopped. "I just wanted to make sure that you were all right," she said. "What is all over you guys? Why are you dressed like that? What smells like ginger-glazed carrots?"

"That would be me," said Munch, shooting another carrot from his nose.

I sighed loudly and rubbed my forehead. "As our plans seem to be of such interest to all who pass by here, foul girl, we were practicing for the talent show."

"I thought you were going to do a Funkee Boyz act," she said, tossing her shimmering hair over her shoulder. "Why are you all covered in brown goop? The Funkee Boyz would never cover themselves in goop. It would totally mess up their hair."

"It wasn't part of our act. It was an accident," explained Munch. "We were having a bit of trouble with Mrs. Annand next door."

"Mrs. Annand?" asked Stacy, "I was just on my way to—"

Munch pointed to the guitar that I was still holding and interrupted the foul girl. "But now we have even more trouble. Our instruments are ruined."

Stacy inspected the crushed heap of guitar. "The Funkee Boyz don't play instruments," she said. "They just sing and dance and look super cute."

"They do not even play instruments?" I cried. "Why did you not tell me this before? This changes everything! There is much planning to do."

I dropped the guitar and pulled out my secret plan book. "We need a new plan! Now leave me, all of you. I have much to do and little time in which to do it."

"Do you need any help?" asked Stacy. "I know everything about the Funkee Boyz. I can—"

"You can go," I told her, pointing to the street.

"Okay, Simon," she said. "But if you need any help, just let me know. I'm going over to—"

"I require no assistance, foul girl," I interrupted. "Perhaps your offer of help will be useful to other people. Preferably, people far away from here."

I sat down on the steps and began to work on my newest plan. Stacy turned and headed down the sidewalk. Munch and Ralph followed after her. Their conversation disturbed my deep concentration.

"Wait up, Stacy," called Munch. "We'll come with you. We need to change our clothes."

"Yeah," agreed Ralph, "this pudding is starting to dry and get crusty." He tugged at his pants. "I think I'm starting to chafe."

"Thanks for offering to help, Stacy," Munch said. "I think Simon's just mad that his plan didn't work. And we got hit with a muffin. And fell out of a tree. And smashed our instruments. And got carrots up our noses."

Stacy laughed. "I don't worry about that. I think Simon's funny. He's always working on those crazy plans. And, seriously, who else reads the dictionary for fun?"

"I know," Ralph said. "I usually don't know what the heck he's talking about, but it's always fun doing stuff with him. Except when he yells, 'SILENCE!' That isn't fun. It hurts my eardrums. I have very sensitive hearing."

"Yeah. Simon's plans are usually—HEY! Candy!" cried Munch. He bent down and peeled a sandy, purple glob off the sidewalk.

He brushed some of the ants off it and held it out to Stacy. "Want a bite?" he asked.

"I don't think so," said Stacy, backing away. "I've got to get going. See you guys."

Munch took a large bite of the purple glob and chewed. "Mmmm. Gritty and sour with a tangy, lean flavor and a muted suggestion of grape. My favorite. Let's head over to your house and grab a snack, Ralph."

Ralph looked down at the mess covering his clothes. "What about this?" he whined.

"Oh, yeah!" Munch said. He grabbed his shirt and started sucking pudding out of it. "I guess we won't need a snack after all."

Chapter 13
Some Stars Are Reborn

"What is that brown mess all over the backyard?" asked my father at dinner.

"Pudding!" squeaked Spencer.

"In fact," I said, "Simon 2.0 is correct. My years of training him have yielded results. He is brilliant beyond his age. That disaster is Aunt Fluffy's most recent attempt at cooking."

"And why is it all over the backyard?" my mother asked.

"We had a slight mishap during the course of our rehearsal today," I explained.

Victoria laughed her evil older-sister laugh. "Oh, yeah. How's your little doofus band going, Simon?"

I glared at Victoria, but once again I failed to make her burst into flames. I do not even know which muscles I need to flex to achieve **combustion**. I will continue practicing until I am successful.

"Our band is about to win a prize of untold riches. We will soon be the most famous musical act on the planet. And you will soon be dog food. Fido! Attack!"

I pointed to Victoria, but Fido remained seated, licking his paws and purring softly.

"What a doofus," mumbled Victoria.

"You weren't bothering Mrs. Annand again, were

you, Simon?" asked my father. "She seems like a sweet lady."

"I cannot understand why anyone would refer to that **superannuated sociopath** as 'sweet.' She is a savage madwoman who uses her dangerous muffins as weapons to crush our artistic expression."

"Dangerous muffins?" asked Mother.

"Muffins!" squealed Spencer.

"I assure you, Mother, her muffins should be considered weapons of mass destruction. She gave Munch brain damage by hitting him in the head with one."

"Munch probably got brain damage from sticking his finger too far up his nose," sneered Victoria. "He's disgusting. And I totally can't understand it. His sisters are soooo cool. How did he get so gross?"

"That's enough," said Father. "Simon, Mrs. Annand is not a vicious, savage madwoman. I had a lovely chat with her the day she moved in. She's very active in the community. I don't know where you get these stories about her throwing muffins at you and your friends."

"But she *did* throw muffins at us!" I insisted. "Well, one muffin, at least. But she threw it multiple times. It was a very hard, dangerous muffin. It contained lethal levels of bran fiber. And some sort of dried fruit."

"Simon, that's enough," said Father. "If you're going to keep rehearsing, you'll have to find a new place to do it. Why don't you and your friends go practice at the park?"

I considered this idea. "As much as I object to

being driven out of my own yard by Mrs. Annand's weapons-grade baked goods, I must admit that practicing at the park may be a better option."

"It will be better for me," said Victoria. "It will keep you and your nasty, puking, nose-picking friends far away from the house."

"And I can assure you that the farther we are from you, the happier we will be," I answered.

Chapter 14
The Sweet Smell of Ernie's Socks

"I don't think I can practice today," Munch moaned at our daily meeting before school at The Fortress. "I've got a headache from that muffin yesterday. And I really think she gave me brain damage. I can't remember multiplication facts."

"You could never remember multiplication facts," said Ralph.

Munch brightened. "Oh, yeah! I guess I don't have brain damage after all."

"I wouldn't be too sure about that," said Mike McAlpine, walking up with the two Ernies trailing behind him. "I'd definitely say you have brain damage."

"Yeah," said Evil Ernie.

79

Eviler Ernie just stood there. Everyone looked at him, but he said nothing.

Mike walked over and put his arm around him. "Come on, Ernie. Give it a try. You can do it. All you have to do is think of something mean and say it. Just like we practiced."

Ernie's lip started quivering and tears welled up in his eyes.

"I CAN'T DO IT!" he bellowed. He spun around and ran away, sobbing.

"Now look what you've done," Mike said to us, turning to run after Eviler Ernie.

"Yeah," agreed Evil Ernie, following Mike.

We watched them go.

"Poor Eviler Ernie," said Ralph.

"Poor Eviler Ernie?" cried Munch. "Didn't Eviler Ernie laugh while Mike gave you so many noogies in second grade that you had a bald spot? Didn't Eviler Ernie used to help Mike steal your allergy-free fruit-flavored snack-like products and replace them with his stinky gym socks?"

"Ohhhh," moaned Ralph, "I can still taste those."

"Yeah, I can't believe you actually put them in your mouth," said Munch.

"I thought they were—"

"SILENCE!" I bellowed. "What I cannot believe is that with the prospect of winning millions of dollars in our immediate future, you are discussing the taste of Mike's socks."

"Millions of dollars?" asked Munch. "I thought you said it was a half a million."

"I have revised my estimate," I said. "But the main point here is that we need to practice before the show. My father suggested that we practice in the park. That will place us safely out of Mrs. Annand's **sphere of influence**. And that foul girl informed us that we need not even play instruments. All we must do is sing and dance. This will make our job significantly easier. I have created a new plan."

I held out my secret plan book, but before I could explain my latest brilliant idea, the bell rang.

When we were all settled in our seats, Mrs. Douglass stood up and lifted a towering pile of papers from her desk.

"All right, settle down," she grumbled, even though the class was already completely settled. Several students were so settled that their heads were down and they were having a pleasant morning nap.

"There are 160 days left until I can finally get out of here. This work should keep you busy and out of my hair for the morning. I want you to write letters to the Chambers of Commerce for every town in Florida and request menus from restaurants that offer senior citizen discounts. Then you're going to make a list of the restaurants, arranged according to price."

She dropped the pile of papers on the foul girl's desk. "Please pass these out to your classmates, Abi."

"My name is Stacy, not Abi."

Mrs. Douglass looked at Stacy through her dusty glasses. She shrugged her shoulders. "Whatever," she mumbled, returning to her brochures.

Stacy picked up the entire pile of papers and carried it to the recycling basket.

On her way back to her desk, she stopped and looked over my shoulder. I was hard at work putting the finishing touches on my plan and did not need her fruity scent distracting me from my work.

"Hi, Simon," she whispered.

I ignored her.

"What are you working on?" She leaned over to look at my secret plans.

I covered my plans with my hand and spun away from her.

"Why do you insist upon interrupting my intellectual activities?" I asked.

She backed up a step. "I'm only trying to see what you're doing. I think your plans are cool."

"Oh, me too, Simon," said Mike McAlpine in a squeaky, girlish voice. "I think your plans are wonderful. Why do you hang around with these dorks, Stacy? You could be hanging around with cool guys like me. I'm going to win that talent show."

"Are you still planning to win by sawing Eviler Ernie in half as part of your magic act, Mike?" Stacy asked.

Mike turned to Eviler Ernie. "Did you tell her about my act, Ernie?" he asked.

"He didn't need to tell me, Mike," said Stacy. "My mother is a nurse at the hospital. She was there when Ernie was rushed to the emergency room."

"The emergency room?" cried Mike. "It was just a scratch!"

Eviler Ernie hung his head. "My grammy saw the scratch and she thought it might get infected so she called an ambulance. I went to the hospital and the doctor looked at it and said it was a nasty scrape. He washed it with some medicine that stung. I was sad, so my grammy took me to a craft store to let me pick out some yarn for my next knitting project. I'm going to knit some slippers for my bunny. He's still upset about when you tried to pull him out of a hat."

Mike shushed Ernie. "My act is supposed to be secret, Ernie!" he hissed.

"Well, Mr. Snuffle-Lumps was not happy about being stuffed in that hat," whined Eviler Ernie. "Now he has panic attacks. I might have to take him to a pet therapist."

Mike groaned and dropped his head to his desk.

The foul girl then directed her big, brown eyes toward me.

"So, what are you planning now, Simon?"

I dropped my pencil and sighed. "I am planning a way to escape from your endless questions about my personal activities."

"Simon is making a new plan for the talent show," said Munch. "His neighbor almost killed us with a muffin and you told us we don't have to play instruments."

"Oh," said Stacy. "I've been working on my act, too. I'm going to—"

"Go away?" I asked, hopefully.

"No, Simon. I'm going to—"

Mrs. Douglass dropped her hands on her desk and stood up. "You have work to do," she said. "I expect it to be quiet in here. Do you know how difficult it is to choose a condominium? I have to decide whether it will be painted tan, beige, light brown, or tawny. I need it quiet so I can concentrate." She looked at Stacy. "And if you are through passing out papers, you should be back in your seat, Sylvie."

"My name is Stacy," said Stacy.

"Whatever," said Mrs. Douglass.

"We will discuss this after school," I whispered to Munch and Ralph. "Meet me at the park under the giant oak tree."

Chapter 15
Triple the Tofu, Triple the Treats

I hurried home after school to gather what I needed. I was once again greeted at the door by my Aunt Fluffy. She was not a part of my plan today.

I jumped back and pointed.

"You? Again?"

Aunt Fluffy smiled, "It's delightful to see you again, too, Sweetie-Poops."

"Number One. You must never again refer to me as 'Sweetie-Poops.' Number Two. Same as Number One."

Aunt Fluffy waved her hands. "Oh, Simon, you're always such a kidder. Come on in and have some of my latest creation: Triple Tofu Treats."

"Triple Tofu Treats?" I asked. "If a single serving of tofu is terrible, how can a triple serving possibly be a treat?"

Aunt Fluffy smiled again and led me into the kitchen. "Well," she explained, "Triple Tofu Treats have three different kinds of tofu. They have extra-stringy tofu, extra-spongy tofu, and extra-gritty tofu. You'll love it! Spencer does. Look at him."

Simon 2.0 was sitting in his high chair squeezing the Triple Tofu Treats through his fingers and spreading it over his head. He was painting with it. Twisting it. Mashing it. Smearing it. He was not, however, eating it.

"I have no doubt that your newest creation will serve Simon 2.0 well as a tool to develop his finger muscles. It may even make his hair bouncy and shiny. Not one bit of it, you will notice, has gone into his mouth."

Aunt Fluffy inspected him closely. "Spencer, sweetie, is it yummy?"

Simon 2.0 looked at her. Then he looked at the mess in his hands. "Food?" he asked.

Aunt Fluffy smiled. "Yes, honey, it's food. Try some!"

Simon 2.0 squeezed a large handful of the gray mush up through his fingers and brought it to his mouth. He touched it to his tongue. His face scrunched up and his tongue hung out of his mouth. "Eeeehhh-huuugh!" he squealed. "Compost!"

I smiled as Aunt Fluffy wiped Spencer's mouth. "No, sweetie," she said, "that's tofu, not compost."

"Compost," he insisted, smearing another handful into his hair.

I congratulated Simon 2.0 on his wonderful word choice, but did not pat his gooey head.

I hurried upstairs and gathered what I needed for the afternoon's rehearsal. "I have matters of great importance to attend to this afternoon, madam," I told Aunt Fluffy as I headed out the door with my large bag of supplies. "I shall spend the remainder of the afternoon at the park."

Aunt Fluffy held up a plastic container filled with Triple Tofu Treats. "I packed up a little snack for you to take along."

"I can imagine no circumstance so **dire** that I might, even for a moment, consider eating one of your tofu packed **comestibles**. My associate, Munch, however, has no such **scruples** regarding what he eats. I shall take some of your distasteful **concoctions** to him."

"Oh, Simon," Aunt Fluffy laughed, as I strode out the door. "I'm sure you boys will love them."

When I arrived at the park, Munch and Ralph were in the middle of a deep discussion.

"Are you crazy?" asked Munch, "A box of unsalted, gluten-free, reduced-flavor crackers?"

"I love unsalted, gluten-free, reduced-flavor crackers," whined Ralph. "I might even buy two boxes."

"You *are* crazy," Munch cried. "Simon, listen to this.

Ralph says that when we win the millions of dollars, he's going to use his money to buy a box of unsalted, gluten-free, reduced-flavor crackers."

"What's wrong with crackers?" Ralph asked. "I like them. They usually don't upset my stomach, and the reduced flavor means they won't be too spicy on my sensitive tongue."

"But Ralph, we're talking about millions of dollars! We're going to have millions of dollars and the only thing you're going to get is a box of crackers? Where's your imagination?"

"I said I might buy two boxes."

"But...millions of dollars, Ralph. You can get anything you want!" Munch said.

"I know," answered Ralph. "And I want those crackers. And maybe a can of warm, flat ginger ale. My parents said it might help with my flatulence."

"What do you want, Simon?" Munch asked me.

"I want to practice so we can win this talent show," I explained.

"Yeah, yeah, I know, I know. But what will you do with the millions of dollars?"

"I have considered many uses for the prize money," I explained, "including the purchase of a rocket engine to strap to my hideous sister. I have also considered using my share of the money to construct a secret laboratory far beneath the Earth's crust. I may also use some small portion of the prize money to purchase some unsalted, gluten-free, reduced-flavor crackers."

"Crackers?!?" cried Ralph. "Really?"

"No. Not really," I sighed. "What you two must realize is that there will be no untold riches and world-wide fame if we do not win the talent show. We will not win the talent show if we do not rehearse. We cannot rehearse if you two spend all your time deciding what to buy with your prize money."

I placed my bag on the ground and opened it.

"What's that, Simon?" asked Munch.

I reached into the bag and pulled out a portable CD player, a few magazines, a pair of craft scissors with jagged blades, a bottle of glue, a jar of silver glitter, and a stick of butter.

"Ooohh! Snacks!" said Munch, picking up the butter.

"Not snacks," I said, snatching it away from him.

"Did you bring any snacks at all?" asked Munch.

"Munch, my **omnivorous** friend, there is a time for snacking and a time for not snacking."

"And what time is this?" asked Munch.

"Not snacking," I said.

"Then why did you bring that delicious-looking stick of butter?" asked Munch.

"My father said that eating butter will raise your cholesterol," said Ralph. "And butter makes my tongue all itchy. I use a soy-based butter-like product instead. But that makes my tongue all itchy, too."

"Munch," I said, "I did bring along a snack for you." I removed the container from my bag. "These are my Aunt Fluffy's delectable Triple Tofu Treats."

"Triple Tofu?" cried Munch. "Did she use extra-gritty tofu?"

"She did indeed," I answered. "But these snacks are for when we have finished rehearsing."

"But I'm hungry now," whined Munch. "I don't want to wait until...HEY!" he cried, pointing to the ground a few feet away. "Who'd throw away a perfectly good brownie?"

Munch walked over to a brownish lump in the grass, picked it up, and tossed it into his mouth.

"What are you doing?!" cried Ralph, "That's not perfectly good! If it's on the ground, covered in flies, with a footprint in it, it's not perfectly good!"

"It's not a brownie, either," said Munch, spitting it back onto the ground. "Do either of you have a breath mint?"

"Eeeaaaauggghhhh," gargled Ralph.

Munch wiped his tongue with the palm of his hand. "That was worse than those nasty candies I ate at Ralph's yesterday."

"I told you, those were bath fizzies that I use for my dry skin," Ralph cried. "Who would keep candy in the bathroom?"

"SILENCE!" I demanded, fearing that we would never practice if this conversation continued. "Allow me to explain my new, revised plan."

I opened my secret plan book and spread it out on the ground in front of us.

Chapter 16
Extreme Makeover

"Thanks to that foul girl, we now know that we have only to sing, dance, and look attractive in order to win the talent show. I have done some research about popular music, and I discovered that many of the musical groups today use pre-recorded music during their live performances."

"You mean they're not even singing? Just moving their lips?" asked Ralph.

"Exactly." I said, holding up the CD player. "So I plan to **purloin** one of my sister's Funkee Boyz CDs. Although I must admit to being slightly disappointed that I will not be able to share my brilliant song about Victoria. Perhaps after we are famous, I will share that song with the entire world. For now, we have only to play the CD and move our lips while we dance to it."

"We have to look super cute, too," said Munch, shoving his finger up his nose. "That won't be a problem for me, but you two have got your work cut out for you."

I held up the magazines I had removed from Victoria's room. "I have also researched the latest trends in style and have devised a clever plan regarding our appearance."

I opened the magazines to show several pictures of The Funkee Boyz.

"What do you notice about their clothing in all these pictures?" I asked.

Munch and Ralph studied the pictures.

"They don't have food stains all over the front of their shirts?" said Munch, peeling a scab of dried, crusty gravy off his shirt and eating it.

"True," I admitted.

"Their clothes are all sparkly!" cried Ralph.

"Exactly," I said. "The first thing we need is sparkly outfits."

I opened the glue and began pouring it all over my clothes. I handed the bottle to Munch.

"Is this the kind that tastes like wintergreen?" asked Munch. "Because I could still use a mint."

"It is not for snacking, Munch. It is for style."

"I was just asking," mumbled Munch. He smeared his clothes with glue, then licked it off his fingers. "Nope," he said. "Not wintergreen. More of a nutty flavor with round, salty overtones. Mild, but with a full finish."

He handed the bottle to Ralph, who dumped it down the front of his shirt.

I then opened the jar of glitter and sprinkled it all over Munch, Ralph, and myself.

We stood back and admired each other.

"We sure are sparkly," said Ralph, shielding his eyes. "All this twinkling is giving me a migraine headache."

"We are sparkly, Ralph, but sparkliness alone is not enough to win the talent show. It must be combined with superior personal attractiveness," I said. Once again, I held up a magazine featuring The Funkee Boyz. "Do you notice a common element in all these pictures?" I asked.

Munch and Ralph stared at the pictures.

"Ummmm...no," they said.

"Look closely at their hair," I prompted.

Munch's eyes grew wide. "Why...it's magnificent," he whispered. "Their hair is all messy, but somehow it's gloriously perfect and beautiful and shiny."

"Exactly," I said. "Shiny hair. I have given this matter much thought and have decided that the only way hair could become so shiny is with a generous application of some **pinguid** substance."

"Huh?" asked Munch and Ralph.

"They must use some greasy stuff in their hair," I explained.

I held up the stick of butter.

"So we're going to make some toast?" asked Ralph. "That would be a nice treat because sometimes toast doesn't make me sick. Unless it's raisin toast. Or wheat. Or sourdough. Or pumpernickel. Or rye with those little seeds in it. Those seeds are very hard on my digestion. One time after I ate some rye bread—"

"SILENCE!" I commanded. "We will not be making toast."

Ralph and Munch moaned.

"However, when we win the talent show, you can use your money to buy as much toast as you would like," I told them.

"And unsalted, gluten-free, reduced-flavor crackers?" asked Ralph.

"And crackers," I answered. "However, for now, we must focus our attention on winning the show. And to win the show, we must have shiny hair." I unwrapped the stick of butter and separated it into three pieces. I handed a piece to Ralph and a piece to Munch.

"Now begin styling your hair," I directed. "Use the pictures in the magazines to help you achieve the desired look. And get the butter out of your mouth, Munch."

All three of us smeared the butter through our hair. We pulled and twisted and pushed for several minutes.

"I don't think we really look like The Funkee Boyz yet, Simon," complained Munch. "But we smell pretty delicious. Maybe for our talent, we should just act like buttered toast. Everybody likes buttered toast."

"Buttered toast does not win millions of dollars and become the most famous musical act in the world," I said.

"That's true," said Munch, "but it is tasty!"

"Our new hairstyles are still not complete. Our hair is shiny now, no doubt, but we need that jagged messiness that makes it appear as if we just got out of bed. "

I held up the scissors.

Chapter 17
Problem Solved

Munch snatched the scissors from my hand.

"OH! OH! ME FIRST!" he yelled. "ME FIRST! I WANT TO LOOK SUPER CUTE FIRST!"

Munch held the scissors up to his hair and was about to make a careful cut when a super-dry, rock-hard, fat-free, high-fiber bran muffin whizzed through the air and smashed into his hand.

The scissors snapped shut. A huge, greasy clump of hair fell from his head and got stuck in the glue on his shirt.

"MY HAIR!" he wailed.

Then the shrieking started.

"What is all that sparkling and yelling about? Don't

you know that this is a public park? People come here to relax and enjoy the peace and quiet! Why are you disturbing everybody by sparkling and yelling like that?" yelled Mrs. Annand, stepping out from behind some bushes.

Munch stared at the clump of hair he had cut off his head.

"MY HAIR!" he wailed.

"There you go again!" shrieked Mrs. Annand. "You kids are always disturbing the peace with your noise! I'm trying to watch the birds, so pipe down! All that sparkling and yelling is scaring away every bird in the county! And give me back my muffin. I'm saving that for a special occasion."

Munch inspected the dirt-crusted muffin lying at his feet. Then he picked it up, rubbed it through the butter on his head, and popped it into his mouth.

"MY MUFFIN!" cried Mrs. Annand. "MY PRECIOUS MUFFIN! I WAS SAVING THAT FOR A SPECIAL OCCASION! YOU GIVE THAT BACK TO ME THIS INSTANT!"

Munch held his hand up to his mouth and spit out the chewed-up wad of muffin. "Here you go," he said.

"MY MUFFIN!" wailed Mrs. Annand again. "YOU LITTLE HOODLUMS! WHY, I NEVER! I'LL NOTIFY THE AUTHORITIES! I'LL CALL THE MAYOR!"

She spun around and stormed away.

Munch watched her go for a moment, inspected the chewed-up wad of muffin in his hand, wiped it through his buttery hair again and popped it back into his mouth.

I gaped at Munch as he continued chewing the super-dry, rock-hard, fat-free, high-fiber bran muffin.

"I—I—" I stammered, "I do not know what to say..."

"I do!" said Ralph. "YUCK!"

Munch continued chewing.

"You have removed the greatest obstacle on our path to fame and fortune," I said. "That was brilliant, Munch. Stunning, marvelous, awe-inspiring, and

sublime. How did you devise such a simple and effective course of action?"

Munch continued chewing. "I was hungry," he said. "You didn't let me eat the Triple Tofu Treats. The butter helped, too." He wiped his hand through his hair and felt the giant bald spot on his head. "My hair..." he moaned, rubbing his fingers over his greasy scalp. "Does it look okay?"

Ralph inspected Munch's head. "No."

"I can't believe she made me cut off all my hair," Munch wailed.

Ralph looked closely at Munch's head. "It's not really *all* your hair," he said, "just a huge clump in the back." He picked the clump of hair off Munch's shirt. "See?" said Ralph. "Here it is."

Munch snatched the hair from Ralph's hand. "My hair!" he cried, sticking the gluey clump onto his bare scalp.

"Does it look okay now?" he asked.

Ralph inspected Munch's head once again. "No."

"Ohhhhh," Munch whined, "my head is ruined! This is going to destroy my social life."

"I think picking your nose all the time and eating gum off the bottom of desks has already destroyed your social life," said Ralph. "And the glue on my clothes is drying and making me all itchy. My parents are going to have to prescribe a topical anti-itching cream. And anti-itching creams make me sleepy. And itchy."

"It's getting hard to move," said Munch.

I looked down at my own stiff, glitter-crusted clothing. "I am reluctantly forced to admit that you are correct. Any efforts we make to rehearse will only be hindered by our magnificent, yet sadly impractical, **sartorial habiliments**."

"Huh?" asked Munch and Ralph.

"We cannot practice with our clothes like this," I said, taking out my secret plan book. "We will continue rehearsing tomorrow. I am already developing a new plan."

Chapter 18
The Band, Man!

I marched into The Fortress before school. Munch and Ralph were already there, sitting glumly in the dirt.

"This is wonderful!" I called out to them. "Thanks to Munch, we can rehearse our act without fear of being assaulted by muffins."

Munch and Ralph did not look as enthused as I thought they should.

"What is the matter with you two?" I said. "Do you not realize that the greatest obstacle to our fame and fortune has been removed? By eating that muffin yesterday, Munch freed us from the crushing **tyranny** of that dangerous lunatic!"

Munch jabbed his finger at my face and yelled, "I think you're the dangerous lunatic, Simon!"

This was an event **unprecedented** in our long history together. Munch has never raised his voice at me. He has called me a dangerous lunatic before, but only after the unfortunate—and extremely unpleasant— yogurt incident in third grade. But even then, he did not raise his voice.

"Do you see my head here?" Munch pointed to the large bald spot on the back of his head. "There is nothing good about this. My mother had a fit when she saw this. My little sisters cut their own hair when they were two years old and everybody thought it was adorable. This is not adorable! This is not the handsome, attractive look you promised me. This is not cool."

"Neither is picking your nose and eating it," I answered.

Munch yanked his finger out of his nose. "That's not the point, Simon. I don't want to be in the band anymore. Since the band started, I've been hit on the head with muffin missiles, my guitar has gotten smashed, I've had ginger-glazed carrots rattling around in my sinuses for two days, my head has been covered with butter, my hair got cut off, my clothes from yesterday are covered with dried glue and glitter, and I've had a terrible stomachache ever since I ate that muffin yesterday. I think I'm dying."

"I think I'm dying, too," said Ralph. "I have a terrible rash from that glitter. And the cream my mother put on the rash gave me a worse rash. And shortness of breath. And numbness and tingling in my left leg. I don't want to be in the band either, Simon."

I stared at Munch and Ralph. I was shocked and appalled. "I cannot believe what I am hearing from the two of you. After all this work, after all these rehearsals—"

"After all these concussions," interrupted Munch, rubbing his lumpy head.

"My parents told you that they'll give you a good deal on head X-rays if you buy them in bulk," said Ralph. "And the first one is free!"

"After all that we have been through," I continued, "you both want to quit now? *Now?* Now that the obstacles have been removed? Now that the most difficult parts are over? You want to quit the band? Give up the billions of dollars that we are sure to win in this talent show?"

"Billions?" asked Ralph. "You said millions last time."

"I have revised my estimate," I said. "But the exact amount of the prize is not important. What is important is...actually, the prize is important. But we will never have the opportunity to win the talent show and claim that prize if you quit the band now."

"You'll never win the talent show no matter what, dork," said Mike McAlpine. He strutted into The Fortress, trailed by the two Ernies.

"Yeah," said Evil Ernie.

"Yeah," agreed Eviler Ernie.

I was in absolutely no mood for Mike McAlpine, and it was evident that my glare was not yet operational.

Mike did not burst into flames.

"Michael," I said, "while we certainly have grown to cherish these little chats with you and your **simian** colleagues, at this moment we are in the middle of a rather important conversation, and your continued presence will serve only to slow the intellectual flow of our discussion."

Mike and Evil Ernie stared. "Huh?" they said.

Eviler Ernie stepped forward and cleared his throat. "I believe what Simon is saying is that he and his friends are having a private conversation and would like us to leave."

"How did you know what that dork was talking about?" stammered Mike.

"Yeah?" said Evil Ernie.

"Sometimes, when I'm at my grammy's house—"

"Stop!" said Mike. "I don't even want to hear about it." He turned back to face Munch, Ralph, and me.

"But—" said Eviler Ernie.

"Not now, Ernie!" insisted Mike. "I just wanted to warn you three dorks that you might as well quit the talent show right now so you don't humiliate yourselves. My magic act is so cool that there's no chance anyone else could possibly win."

"Yeah," said Evil Ernie.

"Except you can't use Mr. Snuffle-Lumps in your act anymore," grumbled Eviler Ernie.

Mike spun around. "What?"

"I said you can't use Mr. Snuffle-Lumps in your act anymore. You just hurt my feelings. You didn't even let me finish telling about my grammy and how I learned all those big words."

"But I need that rabbit for my act!" cried Mike.

"*Our* act," corrected Eviler Ernie.

"Yeah," agreed Evil Ernie. "*Our* act."

"Fine!" yelled Mike. "*Our* act. But I need that stupid rabbit for the grand finale."

Eviler Ernie crossed his arms. "He is not a stupid rabbit. He is very intelligent and sensitive, and he has a name. Please refer to him as Mr. Snuffle-Lumps."

"Fine," growled Mike. "Can we please finish this conversation someplace else?" He glared at us. His glare was in need of even more improvement than mine.

Mike and the two Ernies stormed away.

I turned back to Munch and Ralph. "Well?" I asked.

"Well, what?" asked Munch.

"Are we really going to let him get away with such **bumptious** claims? Are we going to be told by the likes of Mike McAlpine that we cannot claim the splendid prize that awaits the winner of this competition?

Are we going to sit back and watch Mike and his two **beef-witted** sidekicks steal the fame and fortune that are rightfully ours?"

"Ummm...I don't know, " said Ralph.

"Of course we are not!" I exclaimed. "This is our chance to finally have our revenge on them. Mike and the two Ernies have tormented and annoyed and irritated us for years. Now we shall humiliate them in front of the entire world by winning this school talent show."

"Oh, all right," grumbled Munch. "But no more hair styles!"

"And no more glitter," said Ralph.

"Correct," I said. "It was foolish of me to be so easily led astray by the glamour of the music world. From now on, we will focus on the act itself. Meet me at my house after school." I took out my secret plan book and opened it to an empty page. "I have a plan."

Chapter 19
What's in a Name?

I was busy working out the final details of my plan as I wandered home from school.

"Hi, Simon!" chirped Stacy, running to catch up to me. She smiled and brushed her silky hair from her chocolaty eyes. "What are you working on now? Another secret plan for the talent show?"

"Yes, foul girl, I am devising another plan by which I can be assured top honors at the upcoming show-case of talent."

"Oh," she said. "I'm going to be in the talent show, too. I'm going to—"

I held up my hand. "What I cannot understand is why you insist on attempting to share your intentions with me. I am preoccupied with my own planning and cannot possibly give any serious consideration to what you are proposing."

"Oh," said Stacy. "What are you talking about?"

I sighed. "I have work to do, foul girl. Go find someone else upon whom you can inflict your bothersome company."

"But I like talking to you," she said. "I get to hear all those cool words you always use. Are you still planning on starting a music group like The Funkee Boyz? I can't wait to see your act. I bet it will be terrific."

I smiled a bit. She was finally beginning to show some evidence of a brain beneath all her luxurious hair. "Of course our act shall be terrific. I have it all planned out to the last detail."

"What did you name your group?" she asked.

I slumped. "What?"

"What did you name your group?" she repeated. "You guys must have come up with a name, right?"

I snapped my secret plan book shut. "Of course we have a name," I huffed. "Why would we not have a name?"

"So?" Stacy asked. "What is it?"

"It is a secret. The name shall not be revealed until the night of the talent show."

"Why not?" asked Stacy.

"To heighten the excitement," I said. "Now leave me, foul girl. I have much to do and the talent show draws near."

"But I didn't even get to tell you about my act yet, Simon."

"That is true," I admitted as I walked up the steps and closed the front door firmly behind myself.

When Munch and Ralph arrived, I was already on the third page of my list of possible names for our group.

"Hi, Simon. Any snacks today?" asked Munch. "The only thing I found to eat at Ralph's house was his dad's old slipper or something."

"That was a scientifically formulated, nutritionally enhanced, allergy-free snack bar," said Ralph. "But they give me heartburn. And a terrible ringing in my ears."

"I say it was a slipper," grumbled Munch. "So what's on the menu, Simon?"

"My Aunt Fluffy is absent today so the snacking options are rather limited."

"No problem," said Munch, grabbing a handful of Fido's cat food and tossing it into his mouth. "I'll get my own."

Ralph moaned. "That's so unsanitary."

"But so tasty," Munch said. "Like a tuna and liver party in my mouth. It has a piquant boldness that stimulates the palate without overpowering the meaty undertones." He scooped a handful of water from Fido's water dish and slurped it. He swished it around in his mouth. "And it makes its own gravy!" he gurgled.

I pushed my secret plan book toward Munch and Ralph. "We have come upon another obstacle in our path to stardom."

Munch dropped to the floor and covered his head. "IS THAT CRAZY OLD LADY THROWING MUFFINS AGAIN?"

I sighed. "No, Munch, she is not. The obstacle I speak of is one of **nomenclature**."

Ralph dropped to the floor next to Munch and covered his head. "NOMENCLATURE?" he shrieked. "NOW SHE'S THROWING NOMENCLATURE? WHAT THE HECK IS NOMENCLATURE?"

"Please get up from the floor and listen to me."

Munch and Ralph cautiously got up and sat at the kitchen table. "It has come to my attention that we are going to need a name for our musical group," I explained.

Munch rolled his eyes. "Well, yeah. Duh."

I pointed to the list in my secret plan book. "I have taken the liberty of preparing a list of possible names for consideration."

"Oh! Oh! I know! I know!" squeaked Ralph. "How about Three Guys from Mrs. Douglass's Room Who Busted Some Moves and Had Muffins Thrown at Them and Fell Out of Trees and Got Their Heads All Buttered Up and Shaved but Then One of Them Ate a Dangerous Muffin and Then They Could Practice and Now They Are the Best Band in the Universe? That would be a cool name."

"Yeah," said Munch, "that's actually kind of catchy, isn't it? I like it. What do you think, Simon?"

"I suspect that with a bit more thought, something even more spectacular may present itself to us."

"Maybe," said Munch, "but that's going to be tough to beat. That's a pretty good name." He held his hand up to give Ralph a high five.

"Thanks," said Ralph, avoiding Munch's cat-food-smeared hand.

"I have some other suggestions," I said, again pointing to the carefully prepared list in my secret plan book. "For example, how about The **Terpsichorean Triumvirate**? It is perfect. It describes us and its **alliterative** use of the letter T makes it pleasing to the ear."

"I can't even pronounce those words, Simon," said Ralph. "How can I be in a group if I can't even pronounce the name? And anyway, sometimes the letter T makes me puke."

"What?" asked Munch.

"Just kidding," chuckled Ralph. "It's actually the letter S that makes me sick, because it reminds me of squiggling. I told you about the squiggling thing."

I looked over my list again. "Then how about Kings of **Kinesthesia**? Or **Syncopated** Steppers? Or The Whirling **Dervishes**?"

"How about a name that people can understand?" asked Munch. "Like The Groovy Guys?"

"Or maybe Three Super Cool Guys Who Are the Best Musical Group in the Whole History of the Earth and Possibly the Entire Universe?" asked Ralph.

"Perhaps we should stick with Munch's idea," I said. "The Groovy Guys has a nice ring to it. It likens us to The Funkee Boyz without inviting direct comparisons."

"Umm...are you saying you like my idea?" asked Munch.

I nodded. "Yes," I said, "that idea was not completely awful. In fact, I think it is a rather clever name."

"Woo-hoo!" yelled Munch, holding up his cat-food-covered hands again. "High five!"

I shut my secret plan book. "Well, it seems that everything is in order and we are completely prepared to take top honors in tomorrow night's talent show."

"Uh, Simon?" said Ralph. "We've spent so much time avoiding Mrs. Annand and buttering our heads and thinking of names that we haven't actually practiced anything yet."

"Hmmm, yes," I reluctantly admitted. "That may be a problem."

Chapter 20
The Sweet Smell of Success

"Good morning, boys and girls," chirped Mrs. Meredith over the intercom. "It's another wonderful day here at Claude Eustace Wodehouse Elementary School, isn't it?"

There was a long pause.

"Isn't it?" she asked again.

"I keep telling you, Mrs. Meredith, they can hear you but you can't hear them," said Mr. Tappet. "It's a one-way intercom."

"Oh, yes. I forgot. How silly of me. Wouldn't it be nice if I could hear them, though? We could start each wonderful day with a lovely little chat over the intercom. I could tell the boys and girls about—"

"Get on with it," barked Mr. Tappet.

"Oh, yes," said Mrs. Meredith. "I just wanted to remind you boys and girls that tonight is the big night—the school talent show! While we didn't have as many people sign up as I had hoped for, I'm sure that it will be wonderful. If you're not in the show, be sure to come to the cafeteria tonight at seven to cheer your friends on. It will be wonderful."

"Is that it?" asked Mr. Tappet.

"I believe so," sang Mrs. Meredith. "Have a wonderful day, boys and girls."

"Get back to work!" barked Mr. Tappet.

The intercom snapped off.

Mrs. Douglass put down the condominium brochures she had been reading and heaved herself up out of her chair.

"At least I don't have to show up for this night of horrors," she mumbled.

The intercom snapped back on.

"And remember, teachers," barked Mr. Tappet, "attendance at this talent show thing is mandatory. You'd better be there or you'll be doing lunch and recess duty for the rest of the year."

The intercom snapped off.

Mrs. Douglass sighed and waddled over to the rolling cart she kept piled with papers. She lifted a towering stack of worksheets from it and dropped them on Stacy's desk.

"Pass these out to those kids, Barbara," Mrs. Douglass grumbled.

"Okay, Mrs. LaPrade," answered Stacy brightly.

"Just do your work," she grunted at the class. "This morning I want you all to calculate how long it takes to get a sunburn at Daytona Beach while wearing different strengths of sunblock at different times of day with different amounts of cloud cover."

She went back to her brochures.

Stacy carried the worksheets over to the recycling bin and dropped them in as the rest of my classmates began their daily routines of napping, reading, and staring into space.

"Are you ready for the big show, Simon?" the foul girl asked as she returned to her seat.

I grumbled and continued working in my plan book. I could not believe how much work remained to be done before the evening's performance.

"Simon's not too happy," explained Munch. "He just realized that with all the planning we've done, and all the muffins we've had to dodge, we haven't actually had time to rehearse our act."

Mike McAlpine laughed. "Oh, that's brilliant. The talent show is tonight and you dorks haven't even rehearsed. I don't know why you hang around with that loser, Stacy! Ha!"

"Ha!" laughed Evil Ernie.

"Ha," mumbled Eviler Ernie.

"Try it with a little more feeling, Ernie," Mike said. "Like this: HA!"

Eviler Ernie hung his head. "I don't feel like laughing.

I'm worried about Mr. Snuffle-Lumps. He hasn't been acting like himself lately. I think all this rehearsing has been too much for him. I think that being pulled out of a hat has ruined his self-esteem."

"Ruined his self-esteem?" cried Mike, "He's a stupid rabbit."

"He's not stupid," growled Eviler Ernie. "He's very intelligent. My grammy says he's the smartest little bunny rabbit she's ever seen. And if you think he's stupid, you can find another bunny for your act tonight."

Eviler Ernie put his head down on his desk.

"Aw, come on, Ernie," pleaded Mike.

Mrs. Douglass slammed her brochures down on her desk. "Mr. McAlpine! I am tired of talking to you about these disruptive outbursts. Do you realize how difficult it is to decide between a pool view and a pond view? If there are any more interruptions you'll be taking a trip to Mr. Tappet's office."

Mike scowled and sank into his seat.

"So what are we going to do?" Munch whispered to me.

I put down my pencil. I did not yet have a workable plan, but I could not afford to upset my associates.

"Do not worry," I said. "I have a plan. Just show up here for the talent show tonight. I will have everything ready."

Chapter 21
Act 1

I peered out from backstage. My parents were seated in the second row of folding chairs that had been arranged in the school cafeteria. My hideous, scowling sister flipped through one of her ridiculous fashion magazines as Simon 2.0 tugged at her hair with yogurt-smeared hands. Evidently some of my training has paid off.

Ralph's parents scrubbed the chairs with sanitizing wipes and put down seat covers before sitting. Munch's mother watched his younger sisters squirm and fidget in their seats.

Mike and the two Ernies were huddled in a corner backstage, preparing for their act.

"Is everything all set, Simon?" asked Munch. "I don't want to make a fool out of myself out there tonight."

"Our present circumstances are not entirely in harmony with my wishes," I admitted, "and I must lay the blame on my hideous she-beast of a sister. She refused to let me borrow a Funkee Boyz CD. I tried to persuade her to change her mind, but my pleading was **futile**. I had to resort to an emergency backup CD."

I pulled a CD from my bag and held it up.

"*Sing-Along with the Silly Squirrels?*" wailed Munch. "We're supposed to go out there in front of the entire school and dance to a song by a bunch of stupid cartoon squirrels?"

"I will admit that the music is not ideal for our purposes, but as Victoria prohibited our use of her CD, I had to resort to Simon 2.0's collection. *Sing-Along with the Silly Squirrels* seemed slightly less horrible than accordion music by a yodeling weasel, or a banjo-playing moose."

"My sisters have all the Funkee Boyz CDs, Simon. Why didn't you ask me?" Munch groaned.

Ralph peered out through the curtains at the audience. "Ohhhh," he moaned, "I told you I get stage fright. I think I'm gonna be sick."

"Wait till we get onstage," suggested Munch. "It might impress the judges."

The curtains swung open and Mrs. Meredith twirled up to the microphone. "Good evening, everyone! I certainly wish that more people were able to come tonight.

I'm sure that if the school lunch ladies had received the recall notice in time, they never would have served that tainted Sloppy Joe meat at lunch today. The janitors have been hard at work all afternoon cleaning and scrubbing the cafeteria, and most of the vomit smell seems to have faded." Mrs. Meredith sniffed and frowned. "Well, some of the smell has faded, at least. Sadly, the large number of students who ate the Sloppy Joes today has caused most of tonight's acts to be canceled, so we have a fairly short talent show for you this evening."

There was a loud cheer from the teachers clustered at the back of the room.

Mr. Alexander, the music teacher, smiled and stuffed an earplug into each ear.

"In fact," continued Mrs. Meredith, "we only have four acts tonight."

The teachers cheered again.

There was a horrible retching sound from somewhere backstage. Stacy ran out and whispered in Mrs. Meredith's ear.

"Oh, dear," she said. "Make that three acts."

The teachers cheered yet again.

"Hey! That puking kid just stole your act," Munch said to Ralph.

"That's nothing," scoffed Ralph. "I can puke way better than that."

"SILENCE!" I said. "There will be no need of your **regurgitating** abilities this evening. With only three acts, we are certain to win."

Mrs. Meredith introduced the first act. "Please help me welcome The Mystical, Mysterious Magic of Mike McAlpine and His Astonishing Assistants."

Mike swept onto the stage, swirling his blue, sequined cape around him. The Ernies, in matching red capes, remained backstage ready to go on.

Eviler Ernie clapped his hands and squealed, "I sewed these capes with my grammy. See how they swirl? We used chiffon so it would be as light as silk!"

Mike untangled himself from the cape and turned to face the audience. There were only thirty people sitting in the cafeteria, but Mike's eyes grew wide and he froze in place, gulping like a giraffe swallowing a watermelon.

Munch was the first of us to figure out what was happening.

"He's got stage fright even worse than Ralph," whispered Munch. "Watch this."

Munch cupped his hands around his mouth. "They're all staring at you, Mike.... Everyone is looking at you...."

Mike grew pale and began to shake. "I—I—I—" he stuttered.

"Did that kid eat the Sloppy Joes?" asked Mrs. Douglass.

"What?" asked Mr. Alexander.

Munch continued, "Look at them, Mike. Millions of eyes staring at you...."

Mike removed his hat with a slow, shaky hand. "F-f-for my f-f-first trick..." he began. His hand was

shaking so hard that he dropped his hat and a fat, white rabbit hopped out.

"Mr. Snuffle-Lumps!" wailed Eviler Ernie, running onstage. "Oh, Mr. Snuffle-Lumps, did that big meanie Mike hurt you?" Eviler Ernie scooped the rabbit gently into his arms and ran off the stage and down the aisle to a seat next to his grammy.

The curtain closed.

Chapter 22
Act 2

Mrs. Meredith led Mike off the stage. "You'll be fine, honey," she whispered. "You just have a seat right here."

She sat Mike in a chair backstage, wiped some of the rabbit poop out of his hair, and returned to the microphone to announce the next act.

"Our next performer is the wonderfully talented Stacy Hebert. Let's give her a big hand."

Mrs. Douglass looked up from the brochures she had been reading. "I think that kid's in my class," she said to Mr. Alexander. "Heather or Ashley or Amanda or something."

"What?" asked Mr. Alexander.

The foul girl walked onto the stage carrying two batons. Her sequined outfit sparkled like fireworks.

Ralph gasped.

Munch backed away from Ralph. "What? Do batons make you dizzy or something?"

"Sometimes. But that's not the problem."

"It *will* be a problem if you get dizzy and pass out before our turn," said Munch.

Ralph shook his head slowly and pointed past Stacy, out into the audience.

Munch gasped.

I reeled back in horror. How could this be? It was impossible.

"It can't be..." groaned Munch.

"But it is..." moaned Ralph.

"Mrs. Annand!" I gasped.

The wretched old hag was crouched in her seat in the front row, directly in front of my family. At Mrs. Annand's feet was a large basket. I waved at Simon 2.0, signaling him to jump on her head and **incapacitate** her. He merely squealed and cried, "Meatloaf!"

"What do you think is in that huge basket?" asked Munch.

"Do you think she might have brought along her laundry so she can fold it while she watches the show?" asked Ralph.

I glared at Mrs. Annand, hoping that in this crucial moment my power to make people burst into flames might finally work.

It did not.

"So we meet again, you **heinous** crone," I whispered. I turned back to face Munch and Ralph. Munch's eyes were wide. Ralph looked even paler and clammier than usual. "It appears that our arch **nemesis** has returned to continue her brutal, muffiny assaults."

"Muffins?" squeaked Munch. "Muffins?"

"What about muffins?" asked Ralph. "What do you mean?"

I pointed at the basket resting at Mrs. Annand's feet. "No doubt she has attended this evening's production with a misguided notion that she can prevent us from claiming the prize. She obviously seeks to ambush us as we perform."

"She's going to hit us with muffins while we dance?" asked Munch.

"I see no other explanation for her attendance here this evening," I said.

Onstage, the foul girl was preparing for her grand finale. She dipped both ends of her batons into a small jar of liquid. She held them up high and used a lighter to ignite them. Both batons burst into flames and she began twirling them faster and faster.

Mrs. Annand turned her head and seemed to look directly at me. The reflection of the flames glittered and danced in her beady, bloodshot eyes.

Stacy finished her routine, bowed, and the curtain closed.

Chapter 23
Dodge. Duck. Dip. Dive. Dance!

"I think I'll be leaving now," said Munch. He headed toward the stage door.

"I think I'll be joining you," said Ralph, following him.

I held up my hand. "SILENCE!" I bellowed.

Munch and Ralph looked at each other.

"But we weren't talking. We were leaving," said Ralph.

"We *are* leaving," corrected Munch. "Now."

I held up my hand again. "Are you actually proposing to abandon this once-in-a-lifetime opportunity to become rich and popular beyond our wildest dreams? After all the planning and preparation? After all the time spent dedicated to fulfilling our dream? After all the many grueling hours of rehearsing?"

Munch leaned close to me and pointed toward the audience. "*She's* out there. Waiting for us. With her Deadly Muffins of Death."

Ralph clutched his stomach. "Ohhh, I'm too young to be killed by a Deadly Muffin of Death."

"So you just intend to give up?" I asked. "You are prepared to forfeit fame and fortune simply because there is an evil, deranged senior citizen in the audience who is planning to kill us with baked goods?"

"All I know is that I don't want to get hit with another one of those muffins. I'm leaving," said Munch.

"Me too," said Ralph.

"Oh no you aren't," said Mrs. Meredith. She swept the curtain aside and pushed us gently toward the stage. "I'm running a talent show here, and most of the performers are home with Sloppy Joe poisoning. You boys are going to perform."

"Unhand me this instant!" I demanded, prying at her fingers.

Mrs. Meredith is much stronger than she appears to be.

"But..." said Munch.

"But..." said Ralph.

"No buts," said Mrs. Meredith. "You're on."

Mrs. Meredith grabbed the microphone. "Ladies and gentlemen, this is our last act of the evening."

The teachers in the back exploded into wild applause.

"What?" asked Mr. Alexander.

Mrs. Meredith turned and winked at us. "See? They love you guys."

We gaped at Mrs. Annand and her large basket. She seemed to sneer at us.

"She's going to kill us..." mumbled Munch.

"With muffins..." added Ralph.

Mrs. Meredith turned back toward the audience. "Please give a warm Claude Eustace Wodehouse Elementary School welcome to The Groovy Guys!"

The audience clapped politely. I turned and whispered to Munch and Ralph. "I have just devised a brilliant plan. Our enemy is ancient and **infirm**. If we can maintain a **frenetic** level of activity throughout the duration of our performance we may be able to successfully avoid the vast majority of her menacing muffin missiles."

Munch and Ralph stared. "Huh?"

"Dance fast so she cannot hit us!" I yelled as the music started.

Sing-Along with the Silly Squirrels screeched through the cafeteria speakers, their high-pitched voices whining like a dozen dentist's drills.

We are the Silly Squirrels.
We run and jump and play all day!
We'll do a crazy dance!
We'll wear some silly pants!
We'll bake a chocolate pie!

We'll fly into the sky!
And then we'll do it all agaaaaaaaaaaaaaain!

We raced around the stage, dodging, ducking, dipping, and diving. We threw ourselves to the ground and rolled. We hopped. We skipped. We jumped. We danced like nobody has ever danced before.

Munch flopped onto his back and spun himself around and around in a circle, waving his arms above his head the entire time. Ralph attempted to somersault across the stage, but got dizzy and veered into Munch, who was still spinning in the middle of the stage. I

darted gracefully from point to point, pausing after each lunge to assume a brilliantly executed ninja-like stance. I was poised on one leg, my arms outstretched in front of me, when Munch and Ralph both rolled into me, knocking me over.

We quickly scrambled to our feet and continued racing around the stage to avoid the flying muffins. We ran and scrambled and scurried until the song ended and we were safe.

We collapsed in a panting, sweaty heap on the floor.

"Is it over? Can we go now?" huffed Ralph.

"Is it over? Can we go now?" asked Mrs. Douglass.

"What?" asked Mr. Alexander.

Munch pushed himself slowly up off the floor. "Is everybody okay?"

"I...I..." heaved Ralph. "I...um...yeah. Actually, I feel pretty good. Except that I think I'm going to puke. Yes. I'm definitely going to puke."

Ralph slapped his hands over his mouth and raced across the stage, his eyes wide with panic. He turned toward the audience. They shrieked and covered their heads.

"Is this part of their act?" asked Mrs. Douglass. "This is awful."

"What?" asked Mr. Alexander.

Ralph gulped and raced around wildly.

"Come on, Ralph, make it a good one!" shouted Munch. "We can still win this thing!"

Mrs. Meredith waved her arms at Ralph. "Come backstage!" she cried. "Come backstage! Don't throw up on the audience!"

Ralph raced backstage, grabbed Mike's magic hat, and puked in it. He handed the hat to Mike, who was still sitting in the chair staring blankly into space.

"Here you go, Mike. Thanks," said Ralph, wiping his mouth on Mike's cape and returning to our spot on the stage.

I looked out across the stage floor and realized something. "Where are they?"

"Huh?" asked Munch and Ralph.

"Muffins," I explained. "She did not throw any muffins."

Chapter 24
The Grand Prize

Mrs. Meredith beamed at the audience. "Wasn't that a wonderful show?"

"Get on with it!" yelled Mrs. Douglass from the back of the room.

Mrs. Meredith cleared her throat. "Our judges have tallied their scores and we're ready to announce the winner. But before we do, I'd like to take a moment to thank all the wonderful boys and girls who worked so hard to—"

"Get on with it!" yelled Mrs. Douglass again.

"…worked so hard to create this wonderful show for all you wonderful people this evening. It's a shame that so many of the wonderful acts had to be cancelled, but I'd like to thank the lunch ladies for the wonderful job they usually do and to remind parents that incidents of Sloppy Joe poisoning are actually quite rare and school lunch is generally wonderful and most often non-lethal."

"Get on with it!" yelled all the teachers.

"What?" asked Mr. Alexander.

"Before we announce the grand-prize winner, I'd also like to thank Mr. Tappet for all his wonderful support and—"

The intercom in the cafeteria snapped on and Mr. Tappet's voice boomed from the speaker. "Get on with it!"

One of the judges rose from the front row and handed Mrs. Meredith an envelope.

"Our grand-prize winner this evening, who will take home a coupon for a free month of school lunch, is…" She opened the envelope. "Stacy Hebert!"

"What?" yelled Munch.

"What?" yelled Ralph.

"What?" yelled Mr. Alexander.

The foul girl walked out onstage and shook Mrs. Meredith's hand. "Thank you," she said, taking the coupon from Mrs. Meredith and eyeing it suspiciously.

"Our second-prize winner this evening, who will take home a gift generously donated by a member of the community, is…The Groovy Guys!"

We peered cautiously out from backstage. Our families were applauding loudly. Except for my hideous sister. She was trying to wipe the yogurt out of her hair with a page she had ripped from her magazine.

Mrs. Annand was sitting in her seat staring at us.

We did not move.

Mrs. Meredith clutched my arm and dragged me onstage. I dragged Munch and Ralph along with me. "And presenting the prize that she generously donated is Mrs. Annand!"

Mrs. Annand rose to her feet and lifted the large basket onto her arm. She staggered onstage, the weight of the basket causing her to totter back and forth up the stairs.

"These are my moist, delicious, light and airy bran muffins," she announced, handing the basket to me. "I told you I was saving them for a special occasion," she added in a whisper before returning to her seat.

"Muffins? Our prize is muffins?" hissed Ralph as we walked backstage with the muffins. "What happened to the billions of dollars, Simon?"

"Yeah," added Munch, "I didn't go through all that for a basket of nasty muffins. You said we were going to be rich and famous."

Munch handed the basket to Ralph. Ralph handed it to me. I handed it back to Munch.

"I don't want them."

"Don't look at me. I'm not taking them."

"Well, I do not want them either."

Stacy walked over, her eyes sparkling in the bright stage lights. "Hey, guys. Nice job out there tonight. That was a wild dance routine. It wasn't really what I expected when you said you were going to do a Funkee Boyz act, though."

"Our plans were subjected to an unfortunate last-minute modification," I answered.

"Umm...okay," said Stacy. "So how do you like that prize?"

We stared at the basket of life-threatening muffins.

"I went to her house and asked her to donate a baked good as a prize. Mrs. Annand was my mother's home-economics teacher in high school. Her muffins are supposed to be delicious."

"And we would be delighted if you would take them, foul girl," I said, grabbing the basket from Munch and handing it to her. "Your performance was spectacular, although I suspect that it was in **blatant** violation of several fire safety codes."

"That's very sweet of you, Simon," she said. She turned to Munch and Ralph. "I told you he was sweet."

"Sweeter than those nasty muffins, at least," mumbled Munch.

"I am certain the muffins will serve as a delightful accompaniment to the mouthwatering school lunches you have won," I told her.

"Eewww," said Stacy, wrinkling her button-like nose. "You think I'd really eat those poisonous Sloppy Joes? I gave my coupon to Mike." She pointed at Mike, still sitting motionless in the chair at the side of the stage.

The school lunch coupon was sticking out of his hat.

Evil Ernie was waving his hand in front of Mike's eyes. "Hey. Mike. You okay?" he asked. "Mike? Mike?" He snapped his fingers in Mike's face. Mike continued to stare blankly.

Mrs. Meredith walked over and quietly escorted them both back to their parents.

"Well, thanks for the muffins, guys," said Stacy. "See you on Monday."

She walked out the stage door to meet her family. Her dress shimmered and sparkled as she trotted down the stairs.

Munch and Ralph hung their heads.

"I can't believe we're not rich and famous," complained Munch.

"And we didn't win billions of dollars," moaned Ralph. "I can't even buy my unsalted, gluten-free, reduced-flavor crackers."

"But," I explained, "we did beat Mike and the two Ernies, as planned."

"That's true," said Munch, brightening a bit.

"And my parents already have a year's supply of those crackers stored in the kitchen cupboards," Ralph said.

Munch smiled. "It was actually kind of fun up there onstage. Especially since I didn't get hit with any muffins. And, as an added bonus, Ralph got to show off his awesome puking skills. That was a great shot, Ralph."

"Thanks," said Ralph, blushing. "It just takes practice."

Munch sighed and jammed his finger up his nose.

"But even Ralph's stunt puking didn't make us rich and famous, Simon. So now what?"

"Do not fret, my dear associates," I said, pulling my secret plan book from my backpack at the side of the stage. "I already have another plan."

Glossary

It is always frustrating when people do not understand me. I try to convince my friends and family that a few minutes each day reading the dictionary will improve their vocabularies tremendously, but they choose not to follow my advice.

Perhaps you will have more sense than they do. I have taken great pains to create a glossary to accompany this book. I have even written a sample sentence to show you how the word is used. It is certain to be thrilling reading.

And, I might point out, there are times when it would be best if people did not know exactly what you are saying. For example, when your Aunt Fluffy bakes some horrible, disgusting wheat germ and alfalfa sprout cheesecake, you will likely get in trouble if you tell her that it smells like death on a graham cracker crust. But if you choose your words carefully, you can explain to her that you find the off-putting aroma of her unsavory dairy-based confection redolent of carrion smeared atop a sweetened pastry base.

She will probably thank you and kiss you. Not that you want that to happen, however, so use caution.

Study the following list carefully and commit these words to memory. You will not regret it.

acutely: Sharply or intensely. *I am <u>acutely</u> aware of Victoria's terrible taste in clothes.*

alliterative: When words begin with the same letter or sound. *I enjoy the <u>alliterative</u> qualities of the name Evil Ernie.*

barbarian: A savage, beastly person. *Only a <u>barbarian</u> would choose not to read the dictionary for pleasure.*

beef-witted: As smart as beef. Dumb. *Evil Ernie is not actually even as smart as beef. He is too dumb to be <u>beef-witted</u>.*

blatant: Obvious. *My sister's taste in clothing is a <u>blatant</u> offense against good taste.*

bumptious: Bold and proud. And obnoxious about it. *Mike's <u>bumptious</u> claim that he would win the talent show was nonsense.*

coagulated: Having become thick or solid. *Munch's snack was a <u>coagulated</u> gob of goo.*

combustion: The process of burning. *When the <u>combustion</u> was complete, Aunt Fluffy served her pudding.*

comestibles: Food. *Nothing that Munch eats is considered a <u>comestible</u> by the rest of the world.*

concoction: A mixture of various items. *Aunt Fluffy's <u>concoctions</u> of health foods often make me ill.*

concussive: Having to do with a hitting action. *The <u>concussive</u> crash of the muffin on Munch's head was unpleasant to listen to.*

confabulation: Talk. *The foul girl's constant <u>confabulation</u> irritates me.*

conjuring: Producing as if by magic. *Mike's attempt at <u>conjuring</u> a rabbit from a hat was weak and pathetic.*

convene: To gather together. *We often <u>convene</u> at The Fortress for our planning sessions.*

convey: To communicate a message. *I try to <u>convey</u> the importance of reading the dictionary to my associates.*

cretinous: Stupid. From the noun "cretin," which means "a stupid person." *Mike and his <u>cretinous</u> companions don't actually worry me.*

culinary: Having to do with cooking. *Aunt Fluffy's <u>culinary</u> skill is often in question.*

dervish: A wildly howling dancing person. *Simon 2.0 often dances like a <u>dervish</u> when The Silly Squirrels' music is played.*

diabolical: Amazingly evil. *Mrs. Annand is the most <u>diabolical</u> senior citizen in our neighborhood.*

dire: Extremely serious, usually bad. *Ralph's health is generally in a <u>dire</u> state.*

domicile: A place to live. *I must share my <u>domicile</u> with my hideous sister.*

endeavor: A serious effort or attempt. *Aunt Fluffy's <u>endeavor</u> to create delicious food will never be successful.*

ennui: Boredom. Serious boredom. *The <u>ennui</u> of Mrs. Douglass's class is overwhelming.*

fabricate: To concoct or invent. Usually with bad intentions. *I would never <u>fabricate</u> words in my conversation.*

flatulence: A release of gas from the intestines. Farts. *Ralph suffers from frequent and unpleasant attacks of <u>flatulence</u>.*

frenetic: Fast and energetic. *Munch's <u>frenetic</u> nose-picking is disturbing to witness.*

frivolous: Silly. Not serious. *I ignore most of the foul girl's <u>frivolous</u> conversation.*

further: In more depth or to a greater extent. It is NOT the same as **farther**. Farther is about distance. The words are not interchangeable. *I will look <u>further</u> into the mystery of why The Funkee Boyz are so popular. Everyone should move <u>farther</u> away from Mrs. Annand when she starts throwing muffins.*

futile: Useless. *It is <u>futile</u> of Mike McAlpine to attempt to beat us in the talent show.*

gelatinous: Having a consistency like jelly. *Munch ate a <u>gelatinous</u> green glob that he found on the floor.*

geriatric: About old people. *My <u>geriatric</u> neighbor, Mrs. Annand, is a dangerous lunatic.*

gustatory: Having to do with eating or taste. *Munch's <u>gustatory</u> bravery makes Ralph sick.*

habiliments: Clothing. This is an old word that nobody uses much anymore. Please try to use it often and make it popular again. *My hideous sister's ugly <u>habiliments</u> are painful to look at.*

heinous: Horrible and disgusting. *I do not understand how Victoria can look at her <u>heinous</u> reflection in the mirror for six hours each day.*

icon: A person or thing that represents a group of similar things. *I like to think that our musical group still has a chance to become a musical <u>icon</u>.*

ignoramus: An ignorant person. Ignorant is NOT the same as stupid. If you are ignorant about something, you do not know about it, but you can learn about it. If you are stupid, you lack intelligence. You cannot learn. *Do not speak to me as if I am an <u>ignoramus</u>.*

incapacitate: To stop something from working correctly. *Hitting him in the head with a muffin was not enough to incapacitate Munch.*

infirm: Not strong. Usually from age or sickness. *Ralph is frequently infirm after watching Munch eat a snack.*

insipid: Uninspired. Boring. Without flavor. *The music of The Funkee Boyz is insipid and dull.*

internment: Imprisonment. This is not the same as **interment**, which means burial. *Our internment at school ends each day at the final bell.*

jocular: Jesting. *I made a jocular remark when Victoria fell into a puddle of mud.*

kinesthesia: Being aware of how your body is moving. *Our gym teacher frequently talks about kinesthesia as he watches us run laps.*

lexicon: A vocabulary. The words you know. *My lexicon is larger than that of my friends.*

machismo: Macho manliness. *My machismo is legendary at my school.*

maniacal: Crazy and dangerous. *Munch's snacking habits are maniacal.*

mephitic: Very, very, very stinky. *The mephitic odor of the Sloppy Joes is sickening.*

monotony: Boring repetition. *I have written this glossary to relieve the monotony of having to explain myself over and over.*

morbid: Unwholesome. *Munch has a morbid fascination with eating things off the ground.*

nauseous: Sickening to look at. Disgusting. This is an

important word to know. It DOES NOT mean feeling sick. **Nauseated** means feeling sick. If somebody says, "I am nauseous," he is telling you that he is disgusting. *My sister's face is <u>nauseous</u>. Looking at it makes me <u>nauseated</u>.*

nemesis: Something that causes a failure or downfall. An enemy. *Mike makes a fairly poor arch <u>nemesis</u>. He is too easily defeated.*

nomenclature: Names for something. *Deciding on the <u>nomenclature</u> for our band was difficult.*

noxious: Poisonous. *My Aunt Fluffy's snacks are <u>noxious</u> and should not be eaten by anyone other than Munch.*

odious: Extremely unpleasant and repulsive. *My sister is <u>odious</u> in every way.*

omnivorous: Eating anything. *Munch's <u>omnivorous</u> habits make him somewhat unpopular at snack time.*

pinguid: Oily and greasy. *Aunt Fluffy's Wheat Germ and Castor Oil Casserole is a <u>pinguid</u>, coagulated mess.*

preceptor: A teacher. *As my brother's <u>preceptor</u>, I have begun giving him daily vocabulary lessons.*

prestidigitation: Magic tricks. *Mike's greatest feat of <u>prestidigitation</u> would be to make himself disappear forever.*

projectile: Shot through the air. *People still talk about the time that Ralph <u>projectile</u> vomited right up into the basketball hoop in gym class.*

propensity: A tendency to behave in a certain way. *Eviler Ernie's <u>propensity</u> for talking about his grammy makes Mike angry.*

purloin: Steal. *Nobody has ever considered <u>purloining</u> a snack from Munch's lunch box.*

regurgitate: To bring chewed food back up into the

mouth. To puke. *Ralph is famous for* <u>*regurgitating*</u> *in spectacular ways.*

reverberation: A sound repeated many times, like an echo or a vibration. *A deep* <u>*reverberation*</u> *rang through the neighborhood when Mrs. Annand's muffin hit Munch's head.*

robust: Strong, vigorous. *Food with a* <u>*robust*</u> *flavor makes Ralph's tongue perspire.*

sartorial: Having to do with clothing. *The Funkee Boyz have unusual* <u>*sartorial*</u> *styles and tastes.*

scruples: Reservations. *I have no* <u>*scruples*</u> *about throwing pudding at my neighbor.*

simian: Resembling a monkey. *I told my hideous sister that she looked delightfully* <u>*simian*</u> *today and she thanked me. She should read the dictionary more often.*

sociopath: A really nasty person. *Evil Ernie isn't smart enough to be a* <u>*sociopath*</u>, *but Mrs. Annand is.*

sphere of influence: The area where someone has power. *Mrs. Douglass's* <u>*sphere of influence*</u> *does not seem to extend beyond her desk.*

sublime: Totally amazing. The best possible. *My plans are* <u>*sublime*</u>.

superannuated: Old and obsolete. Too old to be of any use. *I need to train Simon 2.0 before he is* <u>*superannuated*</u>.

syncopated: Exchanging strong beats for weak ones in music. *The Funkee Boyz are not talented enough to develop* <u>*syncopated*</u> *rhythms.*

tedium: Extreme boredom. *I often end the* <u>*tedium*</u> *of Mrs. Douglass's class by creating fantastic new plans.*

terpsichorean: Relating to dancing. *We never had*

enough time to rehearse the <u>terpsichorean</u> portion of our act.

triumvirate: A group of three powerful people. *Mike and the two Ernies try to be an evil <u>triumvirate</u> on the playground.*

turmoil: Confusion. *We escape the <u>turmoil</u> of the playground by meeting at The Fortress.*

tyranny: Cruel use of power. *Munch ate Mrs. Annand's muffin, ending her <u>tyranny</u>.*

unpalatable: Disgusting to taste. *Mrs. Annand's muffins and Auntie Fluffy's desserts are equally <u>unpalatable</u>.*

unprecedented: Never happened before. *Ralph's good health would be an <u>unprecedented</u> event.*

vexatious: Irritating. Annoying. Frustrating. *I find it <u>vexatious</u> when people do not understand what I say.*

volition (of my own volition): Voluntarily. *I would never eat one of Aunt Fluffy's treats of my own <u>volition</u>.*